Kiss Me in the Snow

RICH AMOOI

To receive updates on new releases, exclusive deals,
and occasional silly stuff, sign up for Rich's newsletter
at: http://www.richamooi.com/newsletter

To Kristan Higgins.
Thank you for inspiring me.

Chapter One

"All I want for Christmas is a hitman," Sophia Harris said into the phone. "I need to get rid of the competition. We'll start with Meryl Streep and work our way down the list until they're all gone."

"So . . . no Coco Chanel under the tree this year?" her sister Chelsea asked, obviously not taking Sophia seriously. "How about a rocket launcher to go with that? The perfect stocking stuffer . . ."

"I don't think so."

"Okay, I'm writing it down as we speak. One. Hit. Man. Hey, do you think I can find him at Bloomingdale's?"

Sophia ignored her snarky sister. "Listen up, this is important. The hitman can dispose of Meryl's body under the Hollywood sign and then—"

"Why not bury her underneath the Prada store?" Chelsea asked.

"You're right. Much more fitting."

Sophia took a sip of her wine and stared into the sparkling water of the swimming pool as she sat on the back patio of her Beverly Hills home. Sophia and Chelsea were as close as sisters could be, talking on the phone several times every day. Some were serious conversations and others were more on the silly side when one of them needed a good distraction. They also visited each other regularly since Chelsea lived just around the corner in a house Sophia had purchased for her after Chelsea had filed for divorce.

"Where was I?" Sophia asked.

"The disposal of Meryl's body."

"That's right. So . . . Charlize Theron is after Meryl. Then Julianne Moore. Then Hilary Swank."

"Okay . . ."

"Anne Hathaway, Gwyneth Paltrow . . ."

"Gwyneth gave you that *amazing* Fendi satchel for your birthday."

"True. Gwyneth can live, but add Natalie Portman to the list. Who am I missing?" She took a sip of her wine, while staring up into the palm trees in the backyard.

"You forgot Kate Winslet."

Sophia almost spit out her wine. "Good catch! She's way too talented for her own good. And add Sandra Bullock and Julia Roberts to the list. Neither of them can be trusted."

"I agree. They're *way* too wholesome, kind, and sweet to be in this world. They should be ashamed of themselves."

"They should!"

It was the perfect plan, really. All Sophia had to do was eliminate the top actresses in Hollywood, then producers and directors would offer her a role that would lead to her first Academy Award nomination.

Sophia was one of Hollywood's highest paid actresses, known for her action movies. Like a female Tom Cruise. Only taller.

But her action films weren't going to get her an Oscar nomination. She needed a serious role. The problem was Hollywood had pigeonholed her into the action category and wouldn't let her out. Nobody wanted to take a chance on her with a dramatic part even though she knew she had the acting chops to pull it off.

Sophia sighed. "I'm crazy, right?"

"Maybe . . . Have you had anything to drink? We could blame this little episode on the alcohol if it ever goes to court."

Sophia glanced over at the barely touched bottle of Massimo Sauvignon Blanc on the patio table. "Half a glass of wine."

"That's nothing. I drink that much in my sleep."

Sophia laughed. "Thanks. I needed that."

"My lawyer's calling on the other line," Chelsea said, a hint of desperation in her voice. "Gotta go."

"Okay, good luck. Call me right back or come over. Love you."

"Love you too."

Sophia disconnected the call and set her cell phone on the patio table, guilt running through her. Here she was complaining about Hollywood not giving her any respect when her sister was going through something far worse. The divorce from hell.

Sophia stared up into the palm trees in the backyard, thinking.

She wanted that Oscar more than anything in the world, more than even multiple orgasms—although truthfully she was sure she would have a giant O if she were ever nominated. She'd worked her butt off to get where she was today and she deserved it—the Oscar, not the orgasm, although technically the Oscar was a giant O, too.

Sophia had even envisioned the awards ceremony and how it would unfold.

"And the Academy Award for actress in a leading role goes to . . ." Tom Hanks smiled and slid his index finger under the flap of the envelope to open it, pulling out the card. "Sophia Harris!"

Then she'd be escorted up the steps to the stage to accept the award from Tom in a dress Valentino designed for her. Tom would kiss her on the cheek and she would whisper in his ear, "Tell Rita I said hello. Let's do dinner soon."

She imagined she would cry during her acceptance speech, but would pull it all together at the end to thank every single person who had helped get her there. She would make sure everyone knew how grateful she was, then kiss her Oscar on the head and hold him close to her heart as she walked off stage.

Sophia could even picture the award on her fireplace mantel, right next to her *A Charlie Brown Christmas* snow globe and her photo with Steven Spielberg.

Then she would get validation.

Then she would get respect from Hollywood.

Then she would be happy.

Her thoughts drifted to Sally Field and her Oscar win back in 1984 for her role in *Places in the Heart*. Sally's infamous "You like me!" acceptance speech choked Sophia up every time she watched it online.

She glanced over at the caller ID on her buzzing cell phone. It was her agent, Brad.

Sophia had auditioned for the leading role in a drama that would make her a shoo-in for the Oscar, and had been waiting to hear the status from Brad. She knew other A-list actresses had also read for it, but she had given an amazing read. The director had even pulled her aside and told her it was the best he'd seen so far. Still, they should have heard something by now.

Sophia tapped the green answer button on the screen. "If this isn't good news I'm hanging up."

Silence.

"Brad?"

"I'm thinking . . . You caught me off guard with that."

Sophia recognized Brad's serious tone. He was about to deliver bad news.

Again.

"Let me have it, Brad. Who got the part?"

He let out a deep breath. "Kate Winslet."

Sophia squeezed her eyes shut and massaged her

forehead. "God! That's not fair. That woman is perfect! How can I even talk trash about her? And don't you think she's being a tad bit greedy? She already *has* an Oscar! Hold on a second."

"No problem."

Sophia took a sip of wine, deep in thought again.

Hollywood was unfair in so many ways.

Sophia was sure people would think she was crazy for not being happy, considering how successful her career had been up to this point and how much money she had made. She had things most people would dream of: A mansion in Beverly Hills, a swimming pool, a full-time maid and cook, and a fancy German car when she wasn't using a private driver.

Sophia would never have to worry about money, and neither would her sister.

Yet she felt empty.

The Academy Award would make it all better. She was sure of it.

"Brad . . ."

"Yeah, still here."

"The next time you call me, I *would like* to hear you say you got me the role of a lifetime."

"I'm not giving up on you, but don't expect any news the next couple of weeks. Hollywood will be shut down over the holidays, so you'll have to wait until the new year to get that role. Hey, here's an idea—take a vacation. Clear your head.

It'll be good for you. You love Hawaii."

"Seriously?"

"Oh. Right . . ."

Sophia had gone to Hawaii after finishing up production on *Lady Karma 3*, the movie that went on to gross over four hundred million at the box office. They assured her she was in one of the most exclusive, private, Hawaiian resorts, but it didn't take long before photos of her and a waiter were plastered all over the Internet. The tabloids had said they were having "the affair of a lifetime." Ridiculous, since he was a waiter who had brought her a Mai Tai. Nothing more. Nothing less.

Sophia said goodbye to Brad and thought about his advice to take a vacation.

Not gonna happen.

"Hey, sis." Chelsea passed through the sliding glass door at the back of the house into the patio with an empty wine glass. She set the glass on the table and kissed Sophia on the cheek.

"Hey. What happened with the lawyer?"

"Well . . ." Chelsea continued toward the pool, slipped off her sandals and stepped in, the water going just above her ankles on the first step. Then she turned around and smiled.

"What?" Sophia stood and moved toward her sister. "It's over?"

Chelsea nodded.

"Yes!" Sophia hugged Chelsea, happy all the drama she had gone through had come to an end. Her divorce was final. Chelsea's loser husband was now officially her loser *ex*-husband. It hadn't been easy to watch her sister go through that over the last year and a half.

Chelsea's husband had made sure she suffered. He wouldn't agree to any of the divorce terms, even though she wanted nothing from him. They had been unhappy for a while—ever since he changed his mind and told her he didn't want to have kids. Then he cheated on her and the woman was now pregnant with his baby.

That part had been the biggest blow to Chelsea.

"Come on." Sophia led Chelsea by the hand to the patio table. She grabbed the bottle of wine from the table, poured her sister a glass, and handed it to her. "To new beginnings."

"To new beginnings," Chelsea repeated, clinking Sophia's glass and taking a sip of the wine. "Thank you for your support—it means the world to me. I love you."

"I love you, too."

"And you know what? We should go away!"

Sophia blinked. "I don't love you *that* much."

"Oh, come on. I need a change of scenery."

"Plant a couple of trees in your backyard."

"Seriously."

"*You* need what *I* need. A break from men. That's all. We don't have to travel for that because those bastards are everywhere."

"Well, I agree with you, but getting away and disconnecting would do us both some good. A giant Hummer has been lifted off my shoulders."

Her loser ex-husband drove a Hummer.

"I know, but—"

"Please?"

Sophia could see the desperation in Chelsea's eyes and how much she wanted to get away. The woman deserved it after what she had been through. How could Sophia say no? She couldn't. She would do anything for her sister.

Anything.

Sophia sighed. "Before I agree to this, tell me where you want to go."

"My first thought was Vegas, but that's impossible for you since your fans would eat you up. Plus, the last thing I want to do is to get drunk, meet a guy, then rush over to the Elvis Chapel at two in the morning to get married again. Imagine that!"

Sophia laughed. "Actually, that would be funny."

"Not even *close* to funny."

"Let's go someplace quiet and secluded then. Just us and nature and fifty gallons of ice cream. No men."

"Amen, no men! And I'm okay with secluded."

"And *not* Hawaii. Someplace cold."

Chelsea arched an eyebrow. "Do you even *own* a jacket? I don't think you've ever been to a place colder than seventy-five degrees."

"Funny . . ."

"Okay. I'm not going to complain about that. Cold it is. It'll feel more like Christmas if we have snow around us anyway, right?" She gestured around the backyard. "It really is difficult to get into the holiday spirit when I'm sweating and it's almost eighty degrees outside." She snapped her fingers. "Hey, you've always wanted to learn how to ski. Let's go to Bear Mountain!"

Sophia shook her head. "We need to go somewhere *farther* away from Los Angeles where there's no chance of running into actors or paparazzi. Nothing in Southern California, Aspen, Vail, or Park City."

"Swiss Alps?"

"Too far."

"Fine. Hang on . . ." She pulled out her phone, typed in a few words and then scrolled. "Got it. Lake Tahoe."

Sophia thought about it for a moment. "That's not a bad idea at all." She nodded. "Okay. Sounds good—I'm in."

"Yay! Can we take the jet?"

Sophia had access to a private jet when she traveled, to help her avoid the crowds.

"Please say yes." Chelsea leaned in and waited for Sophia to respond.

"Of course. I just need to make sure it's available."

Chelsea jumped. "Yay again!" Wine shot out of her glass and soaked the front of Sophia's blouse.

She glanced down at her blouse. "Did you *really* just do

that?"

"Sorry, sis. If it makes you feel better I didn't like that blouse anyway."

"You wanted to borrow it a couple of months ago."

Chelsea studied the blouse for a moment. "That one?"

"This one."

"Hmmm." She crinkled her nose. "Well, I definitely don't want to borrow it now."

Sophia held up her index finger. "Forget about it. You need to promise me we'll stay away from men in Lake Tahoe. I don't care if we see some hot mountain man with muscular legs filling out his ski pants. Promise me. No men. Got it?"

"Got it. No men."

"Good."

Sophia hugged her sister again, looking forward to a little break. Chelsea and Brad were both right. A vacation was much needed, and a break from men was even better.

Yes, she loved having a man around, but they couldn't be trusted anymore after a string of men had used her for her money and her Hollywood connections.

Sophia wanted real love. She wanted a man who loved her no matter what. No matter how much money she had. No matter what she did for a living.

She was sure that man didn't exist.

Chapter Two

Ethan Woods widened his stance, bracing himself for the freight train that was about to hit him. A few seconds later his one hundred and fifty-pound dog—a black Newfoundland named Bear—came charging in his direction from the kitchen. It was business as usual every time Ethan arrived home to his Lake Tahoe cabin.

"Woof!"

Ethan waved his arms in the air at the dog, trying to get him to apply the brakes. "Easy, Bear. Easy, boy. Slow down! Slow! Down!"

Right. Like that would work.

Bear was a smart dog and knew many commands, but *slow down* wasn't one of them. He slammed into Ethan's legs and midsection, pushing him back into the coat rack.

The licking began before the falling jackets, parkas, and hats hit the floor.

Bear licked each finger on Ethan's left hand like they were covered in gravy, then switched over and got started on the right.

An equal-opportunity licker.

Ethan finally lifted his hands away from Bear's tongue.

"Okay, enough with the basting—I'm not a turkey."

Ethan had had another perfect morning giving ski lessons on the slopes at Heavenly Mountain and now had the rest of the day off. Life was good. Even better since Mike and his daughter Violet were coming over for lunch. They were two of his favorite people. Ethan and Mike ran a very successful water sports and boat tours company during the non-skiing months.

Ethan removed his shoes, slipped into his Uggs, and headed to the kitchen to make sure he had American cheese slices in the refrigerator. He was sure Violet would want grilled cheese sandwiches again and he loved making them for her.

After verifying he had cheese, he pulled the vibrating cell phone from his pocket. "Hey, Uncle Al. What's up?"

"Just wanted to see what I can bring over for Christmas Eve dinner."

Just like last year, Ethan was preparing a special holiday dinner for Uncle Al, Mike, and Violet. And just like last year, Ethan had to remind Uncle Al he didn't have to bring a thing. Most likely he would offer to bring pies. The man was obsessed with them.

"You already know what I'm going to tell you, so why do you even ask?" Ethan said.

"That is *not* an acceptable answer," replied Uncle Al. "I should at least bring pies over."

"Like plural? More than one?"

"It's the great American comfort food! Or maybe I should say comfort dessert!" He chuckled. "Anyway, we can't have just *one*. Besides, you can't make me choose between apple and pumpkin."

Ethan didn't want to argue with him. "Fine. Bring *one* pie. That's it. You know Violet is happy with just ice cream and cookies, and I'm not keeping the leftovers. One pie will do."

"No, it won't. Hey, did you know if you lined up all the pies sold at U.S. grocery stores in one year they would circle the globe?"

Uncle Al taught statistics at the local high school and was always spouting off random facts. Still, he was the smartest man Ethan knew and had the memory of an elephant.

Ethan sighed. "One pie."

"Two pies."

Ethan was getting tired of arguing with him about it, but he would give it one more shot.

"Look, Violet is making Christmas cookies. And it's just the four of us—two pies will kill us. In fact, forget about bringing over even one pie. Bring one half of one pie."

Uncle Al scoffed. "No way! Hey, I'll also bring wine coolers, too."

"Not a surprise."

The doorbell rang.

"Woof!" Bear sprinted toward the front door.

"Gotta go. Mike and Violet are here for lunch."

"Okay, sounds good," Uncle Al said.

Ethan ended the call, pushed Bear aside with his leg, and swung the door open.

"Uncle Ethan!" The cutest eight-year-old girl in the world wearing a purple ski jacket and matching purple pants lunged toward Ethan, hugging him. "Can we have grilled cheese sandwiches?"

Ethan laughed. "How did I know you would ask me that?"

"Violet," Mike said, closing the door behind him. "Can we at least get all the way in the house before you make special menu requests from the chef?"

"He's not a chef, Dad. He's Uncle Ethan."

He loved when she called him that. Technically, Ethan was Violet's godfather.

Mike unzipped Violet's jacket, pulled it off her, and hung it up. Then he pointed to the giant pile of clothes on the floor. "Bear again?"

"Who else?" Ethan grabbed the jackets from the floor and hung them back in their place on the coat rack. "Okay, who's in the mood for Uncle Ethan's world-famous grilled cheese sandwiches?"

Violet raised her hand and jumped up and down. "Me!"

"What a surprise." Ethan put his hand on his chest. "Me, too! Violet has spoken, and she gets her way because she's a princess."

"I've got glass slippers."

He lifted one of his feet in the air. "And *I've* got Uggs. To the kitchen we go!"

Ethan's cabin had an open floor plan—the kitchen, dining room, and family room were like one giant room. It was perfect for entertaining.

Not that Ethan entertained much.

In fact, the only visitors he had had in the last year were Mike, Violet, and Uncle Al, at least twice a week, sometimes more when Mike was feeling a little low and needed company.

Mike had lost his wife Kristina to breast cancer last year.

It had been a very difficult period and Ethan had promised to be there for them whenever they needed him. He had even offered for them to move into his cabin. He had plenty of room: three bedrooms, two bathrooms, and a loft. He even had a game room downstairs connected to the garage, complete with electronic dart board, ping pong table and a music system. Mike had turned down the offer to move in and joked he could never live with a man who was so tidy.

Ethan wasn't *that* tidy.

Okay, maybe he was, but that wasn't a bad thing, was it? Maybe it was a surprise considering his dog drooled buckets every week. Speaking of which . . .

He pointed to the green couch. "Bear. On your couch."

Ethan had bought Bear his own couch to make sure he would never sit in the dog's drool again. He had learned from that mistake the first night he'd gotten Bear from a neighbor who had moved to Switzerland.

Bear gave Ethan a look and then took his time walking over to the couch. A few seconds later he plopped down on the couch and let out a deep breath.

Violet grabbed *The Giving Tree* from her personal section on the bookshelf and turned to her dad. "Can I read to Bear?

"Of course, sweetie," Mike said, turning back to Ethan in the kitchen. "I love that she loves to read."

Ethan grabbed a frying pan from the cupboard. "How has she been?"

"Like a rock." He glanced over to make sure she couldn't hear him. She was already busy reading her favorite story to Bear. "You know what she said to me last night?"

Ethan pulled the bread, cheese, and butter out of the refrigerator and placed them on the island counter. Then he grabbed two tomatoes and placed them on the cutting board. "What did she say?"

Mike leaned in. "She said she knows I promised I'd give her double the love and kisses since Mommy was gone, but she would understand if I was tired one day after work and wasn't able to deliver the sugar." He shook his head, looking back at her. "Eight freaking years old."

Ethan arched an eyebrow. "She used the expression *deliver the sugar?*"

Mike nodded.

"That's funny. And sweet." Ethan glanced over at Violet. "She's such a cute kid and *you* are an amazing dad." He slapped Mike on the back. "You know it can take time."

Mike nodded. "I'm okay. I mean, I've accepted her death. It's just . . . I have the hardest time thinking of Violet growing up without a mom. That's important for a girl, you know?"

"Yeah."

He couldn't imagine what Mike was going through, losing the love of his life. Ethan had had a couple of girlfriends, but what Mike and Kristina had seemed to be another level of love.

The real deal.

Ethan wondered if he would ever have something so genuine, so pure. The truth was he'd put women on the side burner and was okay with it. He didn't have any baggage. He had a good life. He had a life without stress. He had his routine and had gotten used to it.

What more could a guy ask for?

It wasn't like Lake Tahoe had many single women to choose from, anyway. Most of them were married or just tourists coming and going during the winter ski season. They would be gone soon, back to their stressful lives in Silicon Valley or wherever they came from. And *he* would still be there in Tahoe, living the dream.

Single, albeit sometimes lonely, but still living the dream.

At least that's what he kept telling himself.

Ethan prepared the grilled cheese sandwiches and placed them on the table. He liked to add sliced tomatoes to make them a little healthier. Violet didn't mind at all since she had gotten used to them at a very young age. In fact she always gobbled up her sandwich.

A few minutes later, Violet smiled after taking the last bite. She inspected the plate, scraped off some melted cheese with the tip of her finger, and stuck it in her mouth.

Ethan grinned. "I take it the sandwich met your high standards and expectations, Princess Violet?"

"What are you babbling about, Uncle Ethan?"

Ethan arched an eyebrow. "Babbling? Where are you learning these words?"

"Grandma."

"Ahhh. Of course. Did you like the sandwich or not?"

"I *loved* it."

Ethan winked. "*That's* what I'm talking about." He pointed to the red box with the snowmen underneath the Christmas tree. "I pulled another box of ornaments from the garage if you want to hang a few of them on the tree."

"Yeah!" Violet jumped up and pulled the box out from under the tree. She lifted the top off and her eyes grew wide. She smiled and sang "Jingle Bells" as she carefully hung the ornaments one by one.

On the third ornament, she stopped to inspect it. "This one is cool. What is it?"

Ethan couldn't see the ornament from where he was

standing. He walked over to Violet with Mike following him.

Ethan held out his hand, and memories of his ex-girlfriend Lorraine came flooding back in when Violet handed him the ornament. He turned it over, deep in thought.

"What is it?" she asked again.

"I know it's hard to tell, since it's so small," Mike said. "It's a little film reel. The movies you see in the theaters are shot on film. And the film is wrapped around a reel like that, but much bigger."

"I know, Dad. I'm not a little girl anymore."

Mike chuckled. "No, you're not."

Ethan could have sworn he had gotten rid of everything connected to Lorraine. He had found that collectible ornament on eBay and had given it to Lorraine for Christmas the last year they were together.

That was four years ago.

Lorraine had been obsessed with Hollywood and knew everything about the top actors and the top movies. She had thrown Oscar parties every year, lavish affairs where everyone had gotten gussied up. She even had an Oscar contest, where guests picked who they thought would win in each of the categories. He really didn't have a problem with it because it gave her so much joy, but it wasn't his thing and he didn't pay much attention to it.

What he'd had a problem with was her cheating on him with an actor she had met at the casino where she had worked. Ethan had suffered a lot back then and even today the thought of what had happened with Lorraine made him a little sad and angry.

"You okay?" Mike asked, a look of concern on his face.

"Yeah," said Ethan. "I'm good. You know I'm over her, it's just . . ." Ethan covered Violet's ears. "Hollywood rubs me the wrong way sometimes, you know? That whole lifestyle where everyone is sleeping with everyone."

Violet peeled his hands off. "It's okay, Uncle Ethan. I know some bad words."

Ethan chuckled. "And who taught you such a thing?"

"Grandma." Violet and Mike said together.

The three of them laughed as Ethan stuck the ornament in his pocket. "Well, this one doesn't need to go on the tree, but you still have many others."

"Okay." Violet grabbed another ornament from the box. "This one is pretty, too."

The guys walked back toward the kitchen and Ethan placed the ornament on top of the microwave. He felt funny throwing it away since it was a collector's item. Maybe he would donate it to someone who might love and appreciate it. It wasn't something to worry about at the moment . . .

Mike put his arm around Ethan's shoulder. "You know what you need?"

"Don't say it."

Mike opened his mouth.

Ethan held up a warning finger. "Don't."

"A good woman."

"I said don't say it."

"You'll meet her when you least expect it."

"Right. *You're* the one who needs a good woman."

Mike nodded. "I'm not going to argue with that—I do. We *both* do. It'll happen. You just watch."

"I suppose they're just going to fall out of the sky?"

"Well . . ."

The light rumble of a jet flying over the cabin got their attention. They both looked up toward the ceiling.

Mike grinned. "Maybe that's them right there. Two women. Beautiful. Sweet. Loving . . ." He slapped Ethan on the back. "Just for you and me."

Ethan snorted. "Right. That only happens in the movies."

Chapter Three

"Take a look out the right side of the aircraft," the pilot said. "We're flying over Heavenly Mountain Resort. You can see the gondola that goes to the top of the mountain. I'm going to circle around and we'll be on the ground shortly."

Sophia glanced out the jet window at the snow-capped trees and mountains below. "Wow. Beautiful."

"Amazing," Chelsea said. "Can you see our place?"

Sophia squinted. "No. It's there somewhere."

"This is so exciting!"

Sophia had found a wonderful house to rent in South Lake Tahoe—a private, secluded getaway, but still walking distance to the ski resort. There were plenty of places to eat and shop. They even had a Starbucks there. Not that they had planned on going out much since Sophia typically had to avoid public places. Still, it was good to know those conveniences were nearby. Sophia had even read online that most people didn't make a big fuss when celebrities came to Lake Tahoe. She was relaxed and ready to disconnect.

Sophia reached over and squeezed the top of Chelsea's wrist, sighing. "This was a good idea."

Chelsea placed her hand on top of Sophia's. "This was a

great idea. I need this and *you* need it even more."

"What are you talking about?"

Chelsea raised an eyebrow.

"Okay, maybe you're right."

The jet landed at Lake Tahoe Airport, and Sophia turned on her cell phone to check for any text messages or voicemails from her agent.

Nothing.

"Put that thing away," Chelsea said, pointing to Sophia's phone. "You promised we would disconnect while we were here and forget about LA for a while."

"I disconnected on the flight."

"Not funny. Let's go. Don't make eye contact with anyone and move quickly."

Chelsea knew the routine well whenever they had to go somewhere in public.

Sophia chuckled. "You sound like Secret Service."

"I don't want to encounter any delays or crazy people."

Sophia wasn't worried about it. She was wrapped up like a mummy, layered well for the snowy weather of Tahoe with her parka, gloves, and beanie. She doubted people would recognize her.

"Over there." Chelsea waved to the man in the black suit holding a sign with her married last name, Paulsen.

"You going to keep using that name or go back to Harris?" Sophia asked.

"I'm not sure yet. I mean, what if I change my name

back to Harris and then meet a guy the next day? Then I'd have to change it again when we get married. What a freaking hassle."

Sophia pulled Chelsea to a stop. "You promised me. We're taking a break from men."

"I *know* that."

"I don't mean a ten-minute break. I mean a *break* break. Look at you—already talking about getting married again!"

"Not *today*, but *some*day I want to get married again. I'm open to it and want it to happen. I also want a houseful of babies. I'm not like you. I need a man around. I *want* a man around."

Sophia did too, but didn't say so.

Men could be a pain in the ass and most couldn't be trusted—especially the men in Hollywood. Still, she'd be lying if she'd said she didn't miss holding hands, having intimate conversations, cuddling, kissing.

Chelsea waved to the man again. "Hi."

The man with the sign stepped forward. "Paulsen party? Heavenly Mountain?"

"That's us."

The driver glanced at Sophia and did a double-take.

Not good.

"You look familiar," he said, cocking his head to the side. "Have we met?"

"No," Sophia answered, looking away and playing with her hair, trying to cover part of her face with it. "Okay, which way?"

He leaned to the side, trying to get a better look. "You sure we don't know each other? Did you go to South Tahoe High? You a Viking?"

"No."

He snapped his fingers. "Kentucky Fried Chicken on Lake Tahoe Boulevard!"

Sophia placed her hands on her hips. "How old do you think I am?"

"Impossible you've met," Chelsea jumped in to take control of the conversation. "Because we're from . . . Latvia. This is our first time in the United States. Lovely country."

The man's eyes shifted back and forth between Chelsea and Sophia. "I thought your jet came in from Los Angeles."

"That was a connection," Chelsea said, grabbing the handle of her suitcase and pulling it toward the exit. "We should get going, don't you think?"

"Of course," the driver said, following right behind them. "Your English is amazing."

"Thank you."

The driver loaded their suitcases into the back of a white Ford Explorer SUV with dark tinted windows, and a minute later they were off toward the resort on Highway 50.

The highway snaked around and ran right alongside the shore of beautiful Lake Tahoe, the largest alpine lake in North America. Surrounded by the majestic Sierra Nevada Mountains, it was a sight to see, although the driver seemed to appreciate the view in the rearview mirror even more, glancing back at Sophia and Chelsea too many times to count.

Sophia grabbed her phone and lowered the window to snap a picture.

"Hurry," Chelsea said, hugging herself. "It's freezing out there."

Sophia snapped a quick picture and raised the window back up.

Chelsea lowered the window, stuck her arm outside, and pointed. "Heavenly Village! Look, the gondola. We need to take that to the top of the mountain."

Sophia laughed, surprised her sister was hanging halfway out the window. "You're like a little kid. And I thought you said it was freezing out there."

"Not from this side of the car," Chelsea said, making no sense at all. She pointed again. "There's a Raley's supermarket." She sat back in her seat and raised the window. "Driver, please stop at Raley's. We need to stock up on food."

"Okay." The driver glanced back in the rearview mirror and raised an eyebrow. "How did you know Raley's was a grocery store?"

Sophia glanced over at Chelsea, eager to hear how she would lie her way out of that one.

Chelsea hesitated. "Well . . . Raley's means . . . *supermarket* in Latvian. Obviously the owners are from our country. We're proud people."

It was the biggest bunch of bull, but Sophia was proud all right. Proud that her sister had acting skills, too.

The driver stopped at the red light. He glanced into the rearview mirror again. "You *should* be proud. It's a great supermarket."

Chelsea patted Sophia on the leg and smiled.

Once inside Raley's, Sophia and Chelsea loaded up on food and wine. Two people glanced over at Sophia in the bakery section and again by the cheeses like they recognized her. Fortunately, they smiled and continued their own shopping. Sophia had also read online that the pace was a lot slower in the mountain communities and people were happier and less stressed.

It was a refreshing change of pace and Sophia felt even more relaxed. Still, old habits are hard to break. While Chelsea was inspecting a box of dark chocolate, Sophia used the opportunity to sneak a peek into her purse to see if she had missed a call from Brad.

Nothing again.

Brad said Hollywood would be shut down during the holidays, but Sophia refused to believe every single person in the movie industry would be on vacation. Her publicist never took a day off.

Chelsea turned around, but Sophia was able to close her purse before her sister saw anything.

"Are we forgetting something?" Chelsea asked.

Sophia shook her head. "I think we're good."

Just before rolling into one of the lines with the shopping cart to pay, Chelsea pointed to the display near the fresh flowers. "Tiny Christmas trees! We need one."

Sophia picked up one of the potted Douglas Firs and inspected it. The trees were small enough to sit on top of a table and were already decorated with tiny ornaments.

Sophia shrugged. "Seriously?"

Chelsea frowned. "Don't you go all bah humbug on me."

Sophia smelled the mini Christmas tree. "It smells nice, but it's so small. I think it's supposed to go on top of a desk or reception counter for some business."

"Who cares? It's cute! And hey, maybe we can plant it in the ground before we go. Wouldn't that be cool?"

"As long as it's not illegal, yes, that would be cool. Okay, let's get it."

The driver helped pack the bags and the little Christmas tree into the back of the Explorer. They headed toward the rental home and were soon in a residential area.

Sophia glanced out the window at the winter wonderland, snow piled high, and surrounding all the homes and pine trees. "It's so beautiful."

Chelsea nodded. "A thousand times more beautiful than Beverly Hills." Her hand flew over her mouth. She glanced up front toward the driver whose eyes were darting back and forth between Chelsea and Sophia in the rearview mirror.

Then his eyes grew wide. "You're Lady Karma!" he continued glancing back through the rearview mirror. "I *knew* I knew you. Latvia . . ." He chuckled. "What a crock of—"

"Watch where you're going!" Chelsea screamed, pointing through the windshield as the Explorer drifted toward the shoulder of the road.

The driver yanked the steering wheel to the left to straighten out the SUV, which caused the back end of the car to slide to the right on the icy road. The car spun out of control directly toward a snowbank as Sophia and Chelsea held on and screamed.

Ethan watched as the white Ford Explorer he'd been following behind for the last quarter mile suddenly slid off the road in front of him, crashing into a snowbank.

"Not good," he mumbled to himself.

Ethan pulled over, put on the emergency flashers, and jumped out. He would just make sure there weren't any injuries and he would be on his way home.

As he approached the vehicle, he eyed the Tahoe VIP Shuttle bumper sticker on the back of the Explorer. The passengers were most likely coming in for the holidays.

The driver got out, cursing. He walked to the front of the Explorer, his head down trying to inspect the damage. "Son of a—"

"Is everyone okay?" Ethan asked.

"Huh?" the driver said, looking at Ethan like he was speaking another language.

Ethan pointed to the SUV. "The passengers? I can call for help if you need it."

"You don't think I own a cell phone?" Now it was the driver's turn to point to the Explorer. "I will lose my *job* over this. I don't care about them!" He kicked the front tire. "God!"

Ethan decided a conversation with the man wasn't worth it, so he gently tapped on the back window with his knuckles as the driver walked around to the other side of the SUV.

The window lowered, revealing a woman bundled up like an Alaskan mummy. "Hi, give me a cheeseburger and French fries, extra crispy."

Ethan chuckled. "I guess this means everything is okay in there?"

"We're fine, but our driver needs to have his license revoked." She pushed the door open and looked down at the ground. "I guess we should get out."

"There's black ice, so be careful." Ethan grabbed the edge of the door with his fingers to keep it open for the woman. "Take my hand."

"Not necessary . . ." She stepped out onto ice, immediately losing her balance and sliding.

Ethan's hand flew under her other arm to grab her, pulling her closer and lifting her up straight. Just like he'd done countless times for his students on the slopes when they had lost their balance.

"Good catch!" the other woman said from the backseat. "Don't forget about me!"

"Of course not. I'll be right there." Ethan guided the first woman toward the dry patch covered with pine needles. "There you go."

She looked up like she wanted to say something, but didn't.

Maybe she was shy.

Ethan glanced up at the other woman still inside the Explorer. "Okay, you're next. Hang on just a second." He worked his way around to the other side of the SUV, but then stopped when the door swung open and she jumped out.

"Ta-dah!" she said, giggling. "I was just kidding. I'm not a damsel in distress like my sister over there. This is her first time in the snow."

Ethan cocked his head to the side. "Where are you from?"

She opened her mouth to answer and shut it again.

Definitely shy. Cute from what he could see of her face. She kept trying to cover it with her hair.

"They're not from Latvia, I'll tell you *that* much!" the driver said. "In fact, you will not believe this." He pointed to Mummy Woman. "*That* woman right there is—"

"Waiting for you to take us to our destination!" snapped

the second woman.

She obviously wasn't happy with the driver's attitude or his driving.

"Don't get your thermal underwear in a twist," the driver responded. "We're not going anywhere with that damage. I need to call the office and file an accident report and unless there's another car in the area it'll be awhile. Why don't you get back in the car and wait while I take care of this? I left the engine running so you could enjoy the heater."

"*So* kind of you," the second woman said, sarcasm dripping from her voice.

The driver pulled out his cell phone and turned his back on everyone to make a call.

Ethan shrugged. "I'd be happy to take you wherever you want to go. Which way are you headed?"

"Wonderland Lane, but we have no idea where it is."

Ethan nodded and held his palms up, smiling. "I *live* on Wonderland Lane. What are the chances?" He pointed to his Toyota Tundra 4x4 with the extended cab. "Hop in. You'll be there in two minutes."

Mummy Woman smirked. "How do we know you're not a serial killer?"

Ethan considered the question and then shrugged. "Would a serial killer live in a house on Wonderland Lane? Maybe Apocalypse Drive or Doomsday Boulevard, but Wonderland Lane? I think not . . ."

"What's your name?" asked the second woman.

"Ethan Woods."

"Nice to meet you. I'm Chelsea and this thing wrapped up in twenty layers of clothing is my sister, Sophia."

Sophia had a cute turquoise beanie that matched her scarf and jacket. Her straight brown hair flowed out from under the beanie and traveled just past her shoulders.

She was a beautiful woman.

Chelsea looked a little like her sister but was taller, and had shorter hair.

"Nice to meet you both," Ethan said.

Chelsea snapped her fingers twice in his direction. "Let me see your wallet."

Ethan blinked, his eyes darting back between Chelsea and Sophia. "Why?"

"I want to confirm that you *are* Ethan Woods and that you live on Wonderland Lane. You seem like a nice guy, but the world is crazy and we need to be sure."

Ethan pulled out his wallet and handed it to her.

Mummy Woman shook her head. "I can't believe you gave your wallet to a complete stranger."

Ethan grinned. "I trust you both."

Chelsea opened Ethan's wallet and pulled out his license. "Ethan Woods, 125 Wonderland Lane. Check. Nice picture."

"Thanks."

She flipped through a few of the other cards in his wallet. "Safeway Club Card, library card and a STAT card." She flipped the card over to inspect the other side. "What's

STAT?"

"South Tahoe Action Team. Kind of like a volunteer firefighter, but I can also be called upon to help with natural disasters or large scale emergencies."

She nodded and looked over to her sister. "He's clean. In fact, it looks like we landed in an episode of some fifties sitcom." She smiled, gave him back his stuff, then pointed to the back of the truck. "We have to get our things from the back. Thanks so much for doing this."

"My pleasure. Let me get that for you." He gestured to the icy ground. "I'd hate for you to slip." Ethan opened the back door of the Explorer and jerked his head back after seeing the cargo. He eyed the large suitcases, bags of groceries, and tiny Christmas tree. "Okay . . . just a few things." He laughed and reached for the first suitcase.

Sophia—Mummy Woman—pushed his hand out of the way. "We're not helpless." She grabbed and pulled her suitcase, then lost her balance.

Ethan tried to grab her, but it was too late.

Her butt hit the icy pavement hard, with the suitcase landing on top of her.

Ethan pulled the suitcase off her and set it aside. Before she could say something else about how she didn't need his help, he grabbed both of her hands and yanked her to her feet.

She stared at him for a second and then brushed off the rear of her pants.

Ethan reached for the second suitcase and—

"Stop! What are you doing?" The driver ran over toward them. "This is against company policy. I can't allow you to do this. It's my job to get you to your destination."

"Is that right?" Ethan asked, then turning to Sophia and Chelsea. "What do you think of their company policy?"

Chelsea smirked. "Your company policy can bite me."

Ethan chuckled and grabbed the next bag. "And there you have it."

The driver walked off, cursing under his breath and making another phone call.

"Hang on." Ethan yanked a towel from the top of the back seat, folded it, and stuck it behind the seats.

"Shotgun," Chelsea called out, eying her sister and jumping in the front seat.

A minute later, Sophia and Chelsea were both seated comfortably in the cab of his truck, traveling toward Wonderland Lane.

Ethan hadn't had anyone in his car the last few years— except his dog, and maybe Uncle Al one time—so he felt the need to apologize. "Sorry about the smell. I have a dog and he rides with me a lot."

"Isn't that sweet?" Chelsea asked, glancing back to Sophia in the backseat.

Sophia nodded. "Yes."

A woman of many words.

Who knew what was up with her? She had this habit of

pulling her hair over the side of her face whenever Ethan looked at her, which was weird, but he wasn't going to judge. Could be a nervous habit. He wouldn't be surprised if she was upset that her afternoon took a turn in a different direction since their driver crashed the car. But he would have them to their destination in another minute and they could relax and start their vacation.

Ethan had forgotten something very important, though. "What's the address of your place?"

Sophia was finally ready to speak again. "1-3-0."

Ethan grinned and glanced back at Sophia in the rearview mirror. "The Barnhart Rental—right next door to me. Amazing place. You'll love it."

Ethan pulled the truck up the driveway, got Sophia and Chelsea's things out and carried them to the front porch.

He pointed to the door. "Okay, you're all set. I have a spare key to your place in case you get locked out. And you probably already know this, but watch out for the bears. Don't leave any food in plain sight." He clapped his hands together. "Well, you two have fun!" He turned to leave and—

"Wait. Just. One. Minute."

Ethan swung back around. "Yes?"

Mummy Woman stared at him like he was crazy. "Please tell me you're joking about the bears."

Ethan took a few steps back toward Sophia. "No joke at all. You didn't know?"

She stared at him again. "Bears? Like *real* bears?"

Ethan chuckled. "Yes, they're real all right—that's why I warned you." He gestured around to the open space between the houses. "The snowpack around the Tahoe Basin is twenty-five percent of normal for this time of year. Because of an unusually mild winter in the Sierra, some bears have chosen not to hibernate or some are just partially hibernating."

She nodded, trying to take the info in.

He continued, wanting to make sure she understood the problem, so Chelsea and Sophia didn't get into trouble. "Other bears don't hibernate if they have easy access to human food, so make sure you cover everything up. I've talked to more than a few people who have seen bears just in the last couple of weeks. You just need to take a few precautions and you'll have nothing to worry about."

Sophia stood there with her mouth open as Ethan turned to go.

Cute.

Hopefully she was smart enough to take his warning seriously. He would try to keep an eye out for them, just in case.

Chapter Four

The rental house had two levels with four bedrooms, three bathrooms, and a separate family room and living room. The ceiling had real logs as support beams and there were two wood-burning fireplaces. Yes, the place was big, but it still had a cozy, comfy, down-to-earth feel to it. Must have been the afghans hanging over the backs of the couches and countless number of pillows. Everything was in earth tones: brown, cream and green everywhere. The place was amazing.

There was only one problem.

"It's freezing in here!" Chelsea yelled from her bedroom.

"I was just thinking the same thing!" Sophia yelled back, pulling sweaters and pairs of jeans out of the suitcase, placing them in the dresser. "I'll start a fire!"

A few seconds later Chelsea peeked her head into the room. "You're not serious, are you?"

"What?"

"Just turn on the heater."

That's the last thing Sophia wanted to do. "You're just saying that because you don't trust me with matches."

"It may have crossed my mind."

Sophia gave her sister a look.

Chelsea had hinted in the past that Sophia wouldn't survive a day in the wilderness since she had just about everything done for her. Sophia had felt a little offended and hurt by the comments.

It's not that she was lazy or incapable of doing things for herself. Sophia just preferred to manage her time wisely and since she had the money for it, why not hire people to do the things she wasn't really into? Like the house cleaning, laundry, cooking food, and gardening, for starters. She loved her garden, but taking care of a one acre property was difficult, and she wasn't a fool.

Sophia stood her ground. "I'm making a fire, got it?"

Chelsea placed her hands on her hips. "This I have to see."

"Fine. Watch and learn."

Sophia marched down the hallway to the wood-burning stove in the main family room. She opened the stove door and looked inside.

Looked easy enough. All she had to do was stick some wood in there, crumple newspaper underneath it, and light it. She'd seen it done plenty of times on television.

She glanced over to the side of the stove at a metal wood basket, but it was empty. Next to the basket was a stack of newspapers and two long lighters.

Sophia turned to Chelsea. "Looks like I need to get firewood from outside. I'll be right back."

Chelsea raised an eyebrow. "You're not going to ask me for help?"

"Nope."

"Good. I wasn't going to help anyway since I have my slippers on now."

Sophia glanced down at Chelsea's bunny slippers and smiled. "I've got this." She grabbed the wood basket and went back out into the cold, making her way down the stairs toward the side of the house. She had seen the woodpile there when they arrived.

Sophia walked along the path that paralleled the steep ravine between both houses. The wood was protected by a tarp and the overhang of the house.

She pulled away the tarp from one side of the wood pile and placed a few of the smaller pieces in the basket. She lifted the basket, making sure it wasn't too heavy.

"Piece of cake," she said, grabbing a few more pieces of wood and placing them in the basket. "That should be enough for now."

The night was dark and peaceful. The air was fresh. It smelled wonderful, but she was feeling the chill, so she headed back toward the stairs.

She had already fallen earlier and was sure it would leave a bruise on her bottom, so she took her time walking with the wood, her shoes crunching on the snow.

"Bear!"

Ethan's yell startled Sophia, almost causing her to drop

the firewood.

She swung around, her eyes surveying the area for Ethan and the wild animal. Too bad it was too dark. She couldn't see a thing.

Ethan's second warning came. "Bear!"

The beam of a powerful flashlight came from Ethan's deck and his yard lit up like a night game at Dodger Stadium. That's when Sophia saw it, maybe fifty feet away in the open area on the other side of the path.

A real *live* bear digging in the snow.

Burying the remains of someone he ate?

The bear stopped digging and looked in Sophia's direction.

Shit.

Ethan had warned her about bears, but failed to elaborate on what to do if she encountered one. Was she supposed to drop to the ground and play dead? She'd remembered hearing that somewhere, but wasn't sure if it was true. Was she supposed to run? She kept her body still and casually shifted her eyes toward the stairs. She wasn't that far away and should be able to drop the wood and run for her life.

The bear moved in Sophia's direction. First tentatively, then picking up pace, almost running.

Just her luck.

Sophia was going to die without an Academy Award.

Her scream echoed through the canyon. She dropped

the wood basket and flew up the stairs, skipping every other step along the way.

A few more steps across the wood planks of the patio, she made it to the front door opening it in record time. She was proud of her agility, movement, and speed.

That Zumba exercise DVD had really paid off.

Once inside the house, she slammed the door, latched it shut, and leaned against it, her chest heaving, completely out of breath and scared beyond belief.

Chelsea ran to the entryway from the other room. "What happened?"

Sophia placed a hand on her chest, trying to calm her breath. "Ethan was right. There are bears out there. I saw one and the big hairy bastard came at me, looking to eat me in one gulp."

"Oh, my God!" Chelsea checked the locks in the door. "That's scary. How do people live around here if there are wild animals like that close by?"

"I have no idea, but I'm ready to go back home."

A loud knock came at the door.

Sophia and Chelsea screamed together.

Sophia slowly moved away from the door and turned back around, staring at it. "Can bears knock?"

"Don't be silly." Another knock came and Chelsea froze, now studying the door from top to bottom with Sophia. "At least, I don't *think* they can knock."

"Hey, it's me! Ethan." His voice was muffled, coming

from the other side of the door.

Sophia sighed and turned to Chelsea. "Oh, thank God. He must have scared the bear away." Sophia unlatched the locks on the door and opened it.

Ethan was standing there.

With the bear.

Sophia screamed again and slammed the door in his face. "He's got the bear with him! What is he doing with a bear? Who the hell is he? Grizzly Adams?"

Another knock came.

Sophia stared at the door and then turned to Chelsea. "I'm not opening it."

Chelsea shook her head. "Don't look at me."

"Sophia. Chelsea. Open up. It's okay."

How could the guy sound so calm with a bear by his side?

"I'm not opening the door!" Sophia yelled. "You've got *a bear* with you! Do you work for the circus or something?"

Ethan hesitated and then spoke. "No, I don't work for the circus. And I *don't* have a bear with me. He's a dog—albeit a large dog—and his *name* is Bear."

Chelsea squished her eyebrows together at Sophia. "You thought a dog was a bear?"

"I did not see a dog!" Sophia said. "I saw a huge monster. It was a bear."

Chelsea opened the blinds and placed her hands on the window, trying to see outside. "Oh, God. That *is not* a bear.

It's a dog!"

Sophia moved next to Chelsea and placed her hands on the window to see better.

Chelsea was right.

A dog sat just outside the door next to Ethan.

Sophia felt like the dumbest person ever.

She scooted back over to the door and slowly opened it. "Hi."

Ethan waved, a guilty look on his face. "So sorry to scare you." He scratched his dog on the head. "Bear was digging in the snow again—one of his favorite balls is buried there. I was just trying to get him to stop, so he didn't bring half the mountain back into the house with him."

Hands on her hips, Sophia gave Ethan a look that let him know she was not happy with almost having a heart attack. But her hard face melted when Bear pulled forward and licked her hand and leaned against her, almost knocking her over.

"Oh . . ." Sophia said, staring down at the beautiful dog that was giving her so much love. "So sweet and . . ." She inspected her wet hand. "Slobbery."

"Bear." Ethan used both hands to pull the leash back. "Sorry again. He's an affectionate dog."

Sophia wiped her hand on the side of her jeans, admiring the dog. "What kind of dog is he?"

"He's a Newfie." Ethan obviously saw the confused look on Sophia's face, so he clarified. "A Newfoundland. My goofy

Newfie, as I like to call him. His size can be intimidating, but these dogs are known for their sweet temperament and slobber. He's a champion drooler."

"You must be so proud."

Ethan nodded and grinned. "Very proud. Anyway, just wanted to apologize." He turned to leave and then stopped, pointing down the stairs to the scattered pieces of wood on the ground. "You were going to make a fire?"

Sophia nodded.

"How about if I bring the wood up for you and get the fire going? To make up for scaring you."

Sophia placed her hands on her hips. "Do I have *helpless* written on my forehead?"

Ethan stared at her, obviously not expecting that response. "Uh . . ."

"Sophia!" Chelsea said, smacking her on the side of the arm. "Sorry, my sister was just released from an institution and she's slowly adapting to being back in society again."

Sophia felt a tiny bit guilty. "Sorry."

She didn't like when men assumed she wasn't capable of doing things for herself. She could do plenty of things men could do. And plenty of things men *couldn't* do. And she knew exactly what would happen if she let Ethan build that fire. She would owe him. She'd had enough of that you-scratch-my-back-I'll-scratch-yours from men in Hollywood. Although it was more like I-scratch-your-back-then-I-expect-you-to-sleep-with-me.

Men were always looking for something—complimenting Sophia or doing things for her, in exchange for their hidden agendas. They wanted her connections. Her money. Her body.

Forget about it.

It wasn't going to happen again. Not in Hollywood. And not in the middle of nature where dogs looked like bears and their owners were sexy as hell.

Chelsea snapped her finger in front of Sophia's face. "Hello? Ethan offered to build us a fire. That was kind of him. Why not let him?"

Sophia shook her head. "Thank you. I appreciate it, but I would like to build the fire."

Ethan nodded. "Absolutely. If you need help, you know where I live."

Chelsea stepped forward. "Thank you, Ethan. That's so sweet of you. Enjoy the rest of your evening."

"You, too."

They watched Ethan head back downstairs and then Chelsea closed the door, shaking her head at Sophia. "What was that all about? He was just being nice. You need to quit lumping all men into the same category. They're not *all* bad."

"You promised we were taking a break from men."

"I did, but that doesn't mean we need to be *mean* to them. Ethan is a nice guy and, oh my God, did you see those powerful legs of his in action?"

"No," Sophia lied. "I didn't notice at all."

Of course she saw his legs flex through his pants when he pulled Bear back to restrain the dog. Those were just the type of muscular legs that would get her in trouble.

Not gonna happen.

"Funny, he didn't even recognize you." She laughed. "That might be a first."

Chelsea was right.

Usually when Sophia met a person, there was some flicker in their eyes when they saw her. A movement in their body, sometimes they tensed up and sometimes their bodies jerked back. Their eyes went wide. A hand flew to the mouth and countless other telltale signs that showed they had recognized her.

Not this time.

Ethan was oblivious to her and who she was, and she was perfectly fine with that.

In fact, she loved it.

Sophia could just be herself and not be judged because of who she was or what she had done on the big screen. It was nice. Wonderful, actually.

"Are you thinking about how good-looking he is?" Chelsea asked, very close to annoying Sophia.

"No. I'm not. And if you like him so much why don't you go for it?"

"I'm not going to go for it because he barely noticed me. His eyes were on you the entire time."

"Right. Look, let's drop it. It's time to build a fire before

I freeze to death."

Sophia went back downstairs to gather the wood, putting it back in the wood basket. The light in the giant window next door caught her eye.

Ethan was playing with Bear in the large room near the deck. He bent down and kissed the giant dog on the head.

Sweet.

She thought about how she had reacted to Ethan's offer to build a fire. Chelsea was right. She was rude.

Most guys didn't have a clue and were just after one thing, but they weren't all like that. Ethan was just offering to help build a fire. And he was the one who had picked them up on the side of the road when their car broke down.

She continued to look up into his family room. He walked over to the Christmas tree and disappeared behind it.

A few seconds later the tree lit up.

It was beautiful, with the twinkly lights and the big white star at the top of the tree.

She shook her head, mad at herself for having forgotten it was the Christmas season. Where was her head? They were three days away from Christmas!

"Clear your head and enjoy your vacation," she mumbled to herself, and then headed upstairs with the wood.

Ten minutes later the fire was going, and she stared at it proudly.

Sophia rubbed her hands together in front of the flames, enjoying the heat. "And you had doubts? Ha!"

Chelsea nodded and put her arms around her sister. "I doubted you, but I must say that is an amazing fire." She sniffed and then looked around the room. "There seems to be a lot of smoke in the house, though. Look." She pointed toward the kitchen where the plumes of smoke hovered under the bright florescent lights.

Sophia glanced around the home at the smoke and then coughed. Then she coughed again.

Then Chelsea coughed. "Okay, something's wrong. Do you think it's the wood?"

"I have no idea, but I agree. Something is definitely wrong."

The flames roared bigger and with that came more smoke.

"Sophia. I don't want us to burn down the house with us in it. Go get Ethan."

"I'm *not* going to get Ethan. He can't come rescue us every time we have a little problem."

"A little problem? This place is smokier than a reggae concert."

"We're grown adults and need to figure this out by ourselves."

Chelsea shook her head. "There's no time. I don't have my shoes on, so *you* need to go get the man now. Either that or I'll open the door and scream fire. Take your pick and decide in the next five seconds. Five, four, three, two, one—"

"Fine."

Sophia glanced around the room again, sighing. It was true—something wasn't right. And breathing in all that smoke couldn't be healthy.

Sophia ran downstairs, across the snow, and up the stairs to Ethan's front door.

She knocked on the door and waited.

A few seconds later, Ethan opened the door. "Hi, Sophia. Come in."

She stepped inside and closed the door behind her. "Sorry to bother you again. It's just—" Sophia caught a glimpse of something huge moving toward her behind Ethan.

It was Bear.

"Woof!"

Ethan flipped around and waved his arms in the air. "Bear, no. Slow down. Slow. Down!" He reached and tried to grab a hold of the dog, but Bear pushed him out of the way and ran into Sophia, pushing her into the coat rack.

All of the jackets and things from the coat rack hit the floor as Bear licked Sophia's hands.

"Bear! I'm so sorry."

Sophia laughed. "It's okay. I'm okay, but I shouldn't be laughing because we have a problem with the fire at our place. The house is filling with smoke and we need your help. I'm guessing a volunteer firefighter would know what to do."

Ethan threw on a jacket and swung open the door. "Let's go."

Sophia stepped back outside as she and Ethan ran back toward her house. No flames were shooting out of the roof, so that was a good sign.

They ran up the stairs where Chelsea was out on the deck, shivering in her slippers. "Hurry."

Ethan pointed to the deck and gave Sophia an order. "Stay here."

He opened the door and ran inside.

Sophia shook her head. "I hope he doesn't stay in there long."

"He's a professional—I'm sure he knows what he's doing. The bottom line is the fire is contained within the wood-burning stove, so there's no way that the house will catch on fire. But we don't want any smoke damage in the house and I don't want to go to a hotel tonight."

Sophia jerked her head back. "Definitely not. This is probably an easy fix, but I don't like that he is in there by himself."

Even if she was taking a break from men, she didn't want to kill them off. She already had a list for her competition in Hollywood and didn't need to make a separate list for men.

Sophia stuck her head inside the door. "You okay in there, Ethan?"

A few seconds later Ethan appeared in the doorway and nodded. "I'm fine. And everything is okay in there. Follow me and I'll show what the problem was." He grinned. "So you don't have a repeat episode."

Ethan went back inside and Chelsea pulled Sophia to a stop. "He's got the sexiest smile," she whispered. "Did you see that?"

"Behave," Sophia whispered back. She saw it. She was trying to block his smile from her mind.

Once inside, Ethan pointed to the wood-burning stove. "These things are amazing and you can heat half the house with one, but there are a few basic things to remember. Number one, make sure this . . ." he reached down and grabbed a lever, "is open. This is the damper and when it's open, it lets the smoke out."

Sophia shook her head in disgust. "Of course. For some reason I thought this was different since it wasn't a chimney."

"They work almost exactly the same." He moved toward the door. "You should be okay, now, although I would probably open the windows for a bit. Cold air will get in, but the smell will dissipate so you can breathe easier. Let me know if you need help with anything else. Good night."

Just like that he was gone.

And once again he didn't ask for anything in return. No phone number. No date. He didn't flirt one bit. Nothing.

Sophia was baffled, shaking her head. "What an odd man."

Chapter Five

Two hours later Sophia and Chelsea sat on their own ends of the couch, wrapped up in fleece blankets, feeling comfortable and content. They had polished off a bottle of wine, some cheese and crackers, hummus and vegetables, a bag of pistachios, and a bowl of chocolate-covered macadamia nuts.

Chelsea rubbed her stomach. "I'm guessing we don't need dinner tonight."

Sophia nodded. "I think you're right." She stared into the fire she had proudly started, thanks to the advice of their neighbor next door. "This is nice. It feels great to relax. I'm kind of in the mood to read."

"I'm all for reading, but not now. What we need at the moment is more wine. If you read you'll think of plots and stories and movies, then acting, then Academy Awards, then auditions, and next thing you know you'll be on the phone with your agent."

Sophia nodded, agreeing with her sister. "Good point. I'll get another bottle." She went to the kitchen and returned to the family room, holding up the second bottle for her sister's approval. "Ta-dah!"

Chelsea held out her empty wine glass. "Tonight, we

disconnect from everything. Tomorrow we can go venture out."

Sophia filled Chelsea's glass and then filled her own, placing the bottle on the coffee table. "I'm okay with just hanging out here all day tomorrow too. And the next day. And the—"

"Not going to happen. *We* are going out. We're in one of the most beautiful parts of the country and we're not going to hibernate like bears and miss it."

Sophia settled back into her spot on the couch and huffed. "According to Ethan the bears aren't hibernating."

Chelsea furled her eyebrows. "You know what I mean."

Sophia just wanted peace, and being around people in public places had never equated with peace.

"Tomorrow we're going skiing!" Chelsea blurted out. "Lake Tahoe looked so beautiful from up in the jet and this is your first time in the snow."

Sophia placed her wine glass on the side table. "Why don't we wait a few days, so I can unwind a little? That way if I ski headfirst into a tree or get buried to death in an avalanche, you can at least say at my memorial I had a wonderful vacation before I went."

"You're not going to die on the bunny slopes. Okay, listen . . . Tomorrow I'll do some ski runs on my own while *you* take a lesson. I'll find the best instructor at Heavenly Resort for you, I promise. Then on the second day you should have enough coordination to at least go down a beginners run and *I* will join you. Maybe even on an intermediate slope. You should catch on quick since you already know how to water ski. It's basically the same thing except you're going downhill."

"Where am I going to get lessons?"

Chelsea waved a hand. "Don't worry, I'll set it up."

"Private lessons."

"Of course, private. You in group lessons is like throwing bloody fish into shark-infested waters. And don't worry . . . I'll make sure the instructor is hot."

Sophia grabbed her wine glass and took another sip. "You think you're funny, don't you?"

Chelsea sighed. "Loosen up, would you? Are you having a good time so far?"

Sophia nodded and smiled. "Yes. This is very nice, although it's cooling off in the house already." She pointed to the wood-burning stove. "I'll get more wood."

Sophia grabbed the metal basket, slipped into her boots and jacket and went outside. She made her way down the stairs toward the wood pile on the side of the house.

Curious, she glanced up at Ethan's home. His Christmas tree was still lit.

"Bah humbug," she mumbled to herself.

The crunching of snow and rustling of branches in between both houses caught Sophia's attention.

"Not again."

Bear was digging in the exact same spot, looking for his

ball. The dog was obsessed, but she wouldn't deny he was beautiful and sweet.

She set the wood basket down on the ground and took a few steps toward the dog, watching where she was going so she didn't slip. "Hi, Bear."

Bear turned and looked at her and then dropped his head back down, digging. He was obviously more interested in finding that ball than he was with socializing with a neighbor.

Odd that Ethan wasn't out there again. Had Bear escaped? Sophia glanced up when she saw movement in Ethan's window.

Ethan waved to her from inside his cabin.

Sophia waved back and then gestured to Bear to let Ethan know the dog was outside.

Ethan glanced through the window in the dog's direction and then disappeared from sight.

"Come here, Bear." Sophia smiled as the dog finally moved in her direction. "Good boy."

He was such a sweet dog. Beautiful. Sophia didn't even mind the drool. She loved dogs although Bear didn't look as happy as he did earlier. Was he upset she interrupted his play time?

Sophia froze.

Oh, God.

It wasn't Bear.

It was *a* bear.

A real freaking live bear!

I'm going to die.

Sophia backed up, trying not to let the bear know she was on the verge of a simultaneous heart attack and pants-wetting.

Ethan rushed from his house to the edge of the deck. A blast from his air horn stopped the bear in his tracks and caused Sophia's heart to play a sped-up rendition of "Little Drummer Boy."

"Get out of here!" Ethan yelled, blasting the air horn again.

Sophia bumped her back into the handrail and screamed. She dropped the wood basket, and flew up the stairs, skipping every other step along the way.

Just like the last time.

Once inside the house, she slammed the door, latched it shut, and leaned against it, her chest heaving. Her heart banged against her ribs; she was scared beyond belief. Again.

Chelsea ran to the entryway from the other room. "God, now what? Another dog sighting?"

Sophia held up her index finger as she shook, trying to catch her breath. "I. Saw. A bear."

A loud knock at the door.

Sophia screamed and jumped, moving away from the door.

She spun around and stared at it. "There's nobody home! Especially if you're a bear!"

"It's me. Ethan. Are you okay?"

Sophia stared at the door, speechless.

Was she okay? What a question! No. She was *not* okay!

Chelsea glared at Sophia. "You're being rude again." She unlatched the door and swung it open for Ethan. "Hey, neighbor. Come on in."

Ethan stepped inside and studied Sophia. "That was a little too close for comfort. Are you crazy?"

"Ha! This is all your fault!"

"My fault?"

"Yes! Who names a dog *Bear?*"

He cocked his head to the side. "What does that have to do with anything?"

"It has *every*thing to do with anything. I mean . . . You know what I mean."

Ethan scratched the side of his head. "Actually, I don't. And next time you encounter a bear, try not to call it over like you want to play with it."

"Next time you get a dog, name it Rover or Fido or Spot."

He stared at her again like she was crazy. "Okay . . ." He glanced over at Chelsea. "Is she always like this?"

"You mean constipated?" Chelsea answered. "Pretty much."

"Hey!" Sophia said, smacking her sister on the arm.

Ethan chuckled and handed Sophia the air horn. "Take this and keep it handy, just in case. I have a few of them."

She took the air horn from him. "I don't get it. You have a high school here, Subway Sandwiches, even a Starbucks. Where are these wild animals coming from?"

Ethan chuckled. "Well, you have to remember the wild animals were here first. And it's not as bad as you think. Yes, there's been a bit of a problem, but most of it has been caused by tourists who leave food out where bears can easily get to it. Naturally, they come back looking for more. We'll be fine as long as we don't have another Bubba."

Sophia had no idea what he was talking about.

"Sorry. Bubba the Bear was legendary—known around the basin for stealing. He broke into fifty homes and even got into a Presbyterian church over in Incline Village. He devoured over twenty jars of peanut butter that were supposed to be given to the poor."

Sophia frowned. "That wasn't very considerate of him."

Ethan nodded. "No, it wasn't . . ." He continued to stare at her. "You're a very interesting person." He squished his eyebrows together and studied her.

Chelsea leaned over and wrapped her arms around her sister. "I agree. She's *very* interesting and the best sister in the world. This is the first Christmas we're spending together in ten years."

"How come so long?" Ethan asked.

Chelsea shrugged. "Just busy with life, I guess . . . me with a marriage that ate my soul, and Sophia, well, she always had a movie to—"

"Watch!" Sophia blurted out, now feeling like an idiot for startling both Chelsea and Ethan. She shrugged, trying to play it off. "I like watching movies, as you can tell. But I also like reading. Reading is good for the brain. How's your brain, Ethan?"

What the hell is coming out of my mouth? Shut up already!

Ethan's eyes darted back and forth between Sophia and Chelsea, then they grew wide.

Great.

It looked like he finally figured out who she was, thanks to Chelsea's big mouth. Nothing would be the same. She had been enjoying being treated like a normal person—even if he thought she was insane—but that was all about to fly out the window. Now came the questions about her movies, her life in Hollywood, the rumors in the tabloids, how much money she made . . . Or maybe he would just cut to the chase like some other guys and ask her out to dinner. Or to bed.

"My brain is just fine. Thank you for asking." Ethan glanced around the room. "I know you just got here, but I think you need more Christmas decorations."

Sophia blinked.

She wasn't expecting that from Ethan. Did he really not know who she was?

Sophia looked around the room and nodded. "It's not a big deal. I'm not celebrating Christmas this year."

"Oh? Why is that?"

"Well . . ."

"She has a few issues," Chelsea said.

Sophia reached over and pinched Chelsea.

"Ouch!" Chelsea rubbed her arm and then gestured to Sophia. "See? She even likes to torture me and *I'm* her loving sister! Not good, but we're getting her help."

Sophia gave her another look. "Are you almost done?"

"For now. Yes."

Ethan cleared his throat. "Well, look. I have a few extra Christmas decorations in the garage. I'll bring them over and leave them on the porch for you."

"You don't have to do that."

"I know. I want to. As the song says, it's the most wonderful time of the year. Maybe celebrating Christmas will help you feel better. You know, with your issues . . ."

Sophia huffed. "I don't have issues!"

Ethan stared at the stubborn woman standing in front of him. Who knew what had happened to her in the past to make her so crabby? Most likely it had something to do with a man, so she wanted to take it out on all males. He wasn't going to ask. Maybe he reminded her of an ex or something. Too bad. It was a shame to see such a beautiful creature so unhappy, especially during the holiday season.

He wouldn't judge her. People had baggage—that was

life. It wouldn't deter him from being kind and doing the right thing. Ethan loved sharing with others, even if they were tourists he'd never see again. Maybe Sophia's sister would be more receptive to his spreading cheer.

He gestured to Chelsea. "What about you? Would you mind if I brought over a few decorations to make your place more festive?"

Chelsea lit up. "I would *love* that! Thank you so much."

"My pleasure." Ethan glanced back over at Sophia. "I'm guessing you're not going to need help bringing up the firewood you dropped at the bottom of the stairs?"

Sophia stood taller. "I can handle it."

Ethan stuck out his chest, having a little fun. "So can I."

"Don't you dare get that wood," Sophia said with a stern voice.

Chelsea smirked. "I dare you to get it."

Sophia pointed at her sister. "Knock it off, Chelsea."

Ethan glanced toward the door and grinned. "I'll be right back."

"No!" Sophia yelled, trying to grab his arm to stop him.

Ethan laughed, opened the door, and ran down the stairs. He gathered the wood in the basket, carried it up the stairs and inside, and placed it on the bricks next to the wood-burning stove.

"That's not funny." Sophia gave him a look. "Why are you doing this?"

"Doing what?"

"Being so nice?"

Ethan crossed his arms. "What do you have against someone being nice?"

"You didn't answer the question."

"Would you prefer me to be mean to you?"

"You *still* didn't answer the question. And yes, being mean would make it a lot easier."

"A lot easier for what?"

"Just . . . easier."

"You're speaking in code." He shrugged. "Look, I've never felt the need to defend my kindness, but I will tell you it feels good to help others. Especially around this time of year. You should try it sometime."

"Are you insinuating I've never been kind before?"

"I thought I was being explicit."

Chelsea snorted.

Sophia turned to her sister, hands on her hips. "You enjoying yourself?"

"Very much so. This is like a reality TV show with a little of Ripley's Believe it or Not. Don't be rude." She pointed to Ethan. "Say thank you to the man before he goes."

Sophia turned back to Ethan and hesitated before speaking. "*Thank* you. How can we *ever* repay you for your kindness?"

"That's the best part." He grinned. "You n*ever* have to. Have a wonderful evening."

Ethan stepped back outside and closed the door before Sophia snapped at him again. He walked back to his cabin, shaking his head and chuckling. He hoped she loosened up because she sure was a pretty thing.

Ethan entered the side door of his garage and grabbed the ladder that hung on the wall. He opened up the ladder legs and a few seconds later he was pulling down boxes from the rafters. He turned to head back to the house next door, but then stopped and looked back up into the rafters at the long box.

It was the artificial Christmas tree he had before he upgraded to a bigger one. It was just gathering dust, so why not let Sophia and Chelsea use it?

He stared at it for a moment before climbing the ladder again to get the box down.

Smiling, Ethan wondering how Miss Bah Humbug would react when she saw everything he was giving them.

"You're going to celebrate Christmas whether you like it or not," he mumbled to himself, thinking of Sophia again and chuckling. How could a crabby person make him smile so much? Maybe because he knew it was all an act.

He opened the Christmas tree box and got to work. The artificial tree was easy to assemble, considering there were only three sections to connect. Ethan pulled the X-stand from the box, inserted the bottom section of the tree, and tightened the screws, so it was secure. He snapped the middle section into place, and then the top. Finally, he pulled and spread out the fake evergreen branches and limbs to make the tree look more natural. The tree had lights already attached, so all they would have to do is plug it in and add a few of the ornaments.

First, he carried the boxes with the decorations and ornaments next door, and climbed the stairs, trying to be as quiet as possible. After he set them on the porch, he went back to his garage and grabbed the tree. He returned and placed it on the porch next to the boxes.

Ethan peeked inside the window, but couldn't see Sophia or Chelsea, so he added one more final touch. He pulled an angel from the box and attached it to the top of the tree.

He stood back a few feet to admire it. "Perfect."

It was amazing how much fun he had when he did things for others. Now there was just one more thing to do. It was time to play Ding Dong Ditch.

Ethan rang the doorbell and then took off running down the stairs. He sprinted across the snow as fast as he could without falling on his face and into the side door of his garage, all the while trying to contain his laughter.

He left the door cracked open just enough to watch the action next door.

The door opened slowly and Sophia stepped outside, crossing her arms and looking around. "What the hell? Ethan!"

Chapter Six

Ethan was wrapping up a half-day morning lesson at the ski and ride school with a group of mostly four and five year-olds, his favorite age to teach. It had been a perfect morning on the slopes, with blue skies and plenty of powder under their feet.

He clapped his hands together. "Great job, everyone! See you tomorrow!"

"Thank you, Ethan!" a few of them said, waving and following another resort employee carefully toward the main lodge. That's where the kids would meet up with their parents, grab a cup of hot chocolate, and talk about their first experience skiing. The brave ones took the lift back up with their parents to test their newly learned skills.

Ethan loved teaching people how to ski. He loved Lake Tahoe. He loved his life.

After skiing down to the clubhouse, Ethan stopped at his locker to grab his bottle of water. A couple of sips later, he closed it back up and stuck it in the locker. He pulled the printout from his appointment folder and checked the name of his next client, who had reserved a lesson through the online registration system on the company website.

Sophia.

He stared at the first name and smiled, thinking of his lovely neighbor next door. That would be a lot of fun to give *her* a lesson. But he knew there was no way it could be *that* Sophia. She was way too stubborn to take lessons and would insist learning on her own.

He closed the locker and skied to the clock tower to wait for his student. Typically most of his lessons were done in groups and most people were okay with that because the private lessons were almost five times more expensive. The website mentioned for the client to meet the instructor at the clock tower and to look for the instructor's bright red jacket.

"Excuse me?" called the familiar female voice behind him.

No way.

He turned around and there she was. Miss Stubborn. The woman he was just thinking about. It looked like his day just got even better.

Sophia yanked the goggles off her head, pulling a clump of hair with it. "Ouch!" She untangled the goggles and then eyed his instructor jacket. "Is this some kind of joke?"

"Joke? Not at all." Ethan grinned. "Fate? Absolutely."

A young girl walked by, smiling and waving to Sophia.

Sophia waved back.

Ethan raised an eyebrow.

"There are some nice people in Lake Tahoe," Sophia said.

"Ahhh . . . I get it. It's okay for kids to be nice to you, but not adults."

"Basically. Can we get the lesson started?"

"Of course. Follow me."

Sophia followed Ethan up the slope to an open area roped off for private lessons. He pulled the rope up so they both could walk to the other side, then turned around, careful not to look at her body again.

"Okay," he said, keeping eye contact with her. "How much do you know? Are you a *beginner* beginner?"

"I know how to water ski, if that helps."

"It helps a lot." He studied her for a few seconds. "But let's get one thing clear right now."

She placed her hands on her hips. "What?"

"I will teach you how to ski. During the lessons it may appear that I'm being kind and helpful. Just go with it. If it makes it easier, pretend I'm only being nice because it's part of my job."

"You're really something, you know that?"

He grinned. "Thanks for noticing."

Ethan was cute as hell and just the type of guy who had too often gotten Sophia into trouble in Hollywood. Tall. Dark. Handsome. Confident. Amazing body. Heart-stopping smile.

Trouble.

Sophia needed to kill any thoughts of his yumminess ASAP. She pictured him as a smelly grotesque man with scars on his face, pimples, greasy hair and an exploding beer belly.

Nope. Didn't work.

Damn!

She needed to focus on his ski instruction. Her goal was to feel confident enough to join Chelsea skiing on the slopes tomorrow. That was it. The last thing she needed was to break a leg or ski off a cliff because she was more focused on his chiseled jaw and cute butt.

"Sophia?"

Concentrate. You can do it. "Yes?"

"I wanted to make sure you heard what I said because it's *very* important."

She searched her brain trying to remember any words that came from his sexy mouth. There was something about gliding on straight runs and performing consistent link turns, but the rest was all a blur.

"Sorry, I was a little distracted," she admitted. She had no intention of telling him he was the object of her distraction. "Please tell me again."

"No problem." He repeated the instructions and then said, "Got it?"

"Got it," she replied.

"Good. Lock your skis into your bindings and follow me."

Sophia followed his instructions and glided behind him down the slope without any problems. Knowing how to waterski really helped because she was feeling confident on the snow. A little too confident, maybe.

She hit a small bump and lost her balance, her arms flailing in the air before falling back and landing on her butt and elbows. Good thing the snow was soft. It didn't hurt, but she could feel the cold of the snow against her backside.

Ethan skied over and reached out his hand. "Nice try."

She reached for his hand and he pulled her to her feet in one swift motion.

Sophia wobbled and Ethan grabbed her by the waist to steady her with his firm grip.

She looked up but he didn't say a word.

What was the man thinking?

He cleared his throat. "You're doing great. Don't forget to bend your knees and don't be afraid to lean forward. It'll give you more stability."

"Okay . . ."

He showed her some other techniques and tricks and she copied all of them. Perfectly. Next, he skied ahead of her to the bottom of the slope, doing the perfect hockey stop.

He turned and waited. It was Sophia's turn.

Talk about pressure.

She took her time heading down toward Ethan, side-stepping and trying to remember the proper utilization of the poles, at the same time knowing there was a man who was watching her every move.

Sophia skied to the bottom and turned slightly to stop, surprising herself.

"Great," Ethan said, nodding his approval. "You're a natural."

"Thanks. I guess learning to waterski paid off."

"It did. You've got all the basics down and even some intermediate techniques because of your experience on the water. I'll be honest, you probably didn't even need this lesson." He chuckled. "You sure you want to continue?"

Who was this guy? Sophia typically couldn't get rid of men, guys constantly hitting on her and saying anything just to be with her.

Ethan was trying to get rid of *her.*

The man was a freak of nature.

"Did you have a question about something?' he asked.

"Huh?"

"Sorry . . . You looked like you had something you wanted to say."

She shook her head. "Nope. We can continue."

"Okay, then I'll just give you a few more tips, then you can hit the slopes on your own. You don't need me."

"Okay . . ."

The more he tried to get rid of her the more she wanted to know more about him. Who was Ethan and why was he living in a place like Lake Tahoe?

One thing was for sure, she felt confident on skis—

mostly—and that was a great feeling. She looked forward to skiing with Chelsea.

A woman skied by and waved. "Sophia! Hi!"

Sophia waved back, trying not to make a big deal of it. It would be interesting to see how Ethan responded this time. She had no idea how long she could hide who she was, but she was still quite surprised he hadn't had a clue.

Ethan stared at her for a moment. "You seem to have lots of friends here."

You have no idea.

Sophia waved it off. "She looked like the woman I talked to at the supermarket the day we arrived. You know . . . before the car broke down and you rescued us."

Ethan chuckled. "Rescued may not be the best word. I was in the right place at the right time and just gave you a ride. I was happy to help."

She nodded, thinking this may be the perfect time to apologize for being such a bitch.

"About that," she began, wondering how to say it. "Look, I haven't been acting lady-like and I wanted to say I'm sorry."

"Don't worry about it."

"I worry about it, believe me. Yes, I've got things going on in my professional and personal life, but I don't need to take it out on you. The truth is you've been more than kind. Really. I'm not used to it, especially kindness coming from someone who wants nothing in return." She thought about it for a moment, thinking she felt better to get that off her chest. "Anyway, if I become a bitch again, and I hope I don't, feel free to ignore me."

Ethan chuckled. "I'm already using that trick."

"Oh! You're bad." She smacked him on arm and lost her balance again.

Ethan was quick with his reflexes, grabbing her by the arms and pulling her close. She slipped again and he pulled her closer, not letting go. She snaked her arms around his back and pulled tight. No way she would fall now although she had to admit it might look awkward to someone skiing by. It must have looked like they were hugging.

Technically, they were.

Her body was pressed against his. Leg to leg. Chest to chest. It felt good. Great.

Knock it off!

Sophia wasn't supposed to be feeling anything. She was taking a break from men. She wasn't supposed to notice how good it felt to be in his arms.

"I'm okay," she said, looking up into his velvety chocolate eyes. "Got it. Really."

"Okay," Ethan said, not breaking eye contact with her, but letting go of her arms.

She could have sworn they had a connection there. Just a little spark.

Then she fell back hard onto her butt.

Again.

Chapter Seven

Christmas Eve arrived and Sophia and Chelsea spent the morning skiing. The plan for the rest of the day was to grab a quick bite to eat in Heavenly Village, then head back to the house to relax and prepare a special meal in the evening.

Sophia felt different.

She had lost some—or most—of her bah humbug attitude and it felt good. She couldn't help but wonder if it had something to do with Ethan the day before. It had felt good to apologize, and it felt even better to be on the snow with him.

After finishing the last run down the slopes, Sophia spotted Ethan teaching a group lesson and waved to him. He smiled and waved right back.

Then Sophia fell on her butt.

Embarrassed, she picked herself up, dusted off her pants, and turned to Chelsea. "I skied with you the entire morning and didn't fall one single time." She shook her head. "I seem to only fall when I'm around Ethan."

"Did you admit you're falling for Ethan?" Chelsea said, laughing. "My, my, my."

"Very funny."

"But seriously . . . did you see the way he looked at you?"

Of course I did. I'm not blind. "No."

Chelsea popped her boots out of her bindings. "Right. I think he's got the hots for you."

"Ha!" Sophia said, picking up her skis and following Chelsea to the rental shop. "Ethan doesn't have the hots for anyone—especially me. The guy obviously already has a woman in his life or has no interest in women. One or the other—I'm sure of it."

They turned in their equipment at the rental shop and strolled past the shops in Heavenly Village.

Chelsea pointed to the California Burger Company. "There. We need to eat there, like right now."

Sophia stopped and placed her hands on her hips. "I thought we were going to have a light lunch. I'm not eating that entire ham tonight by myself."

Chelsea swung the door open to the restaurant. "We're not eating dinner for at least another seven hours. Besides, I'm in the mood for a beer."

A beer sounded great to Sophia too.

It had been an amazing morning on the mountain. She enjoyed the fresh air, the powder under her skis, and the fact that she had completely disconnected from Hollywood. She knew several people who had left Los Angeles and moved away to slower lives in Oregon, Washington, and Colorado. Now she knew firsthand what they were talking about when they said they were one with nature. There was something special about it, for sure. But wouldn't it get old after a while? She felt exhilarated, but she suspected she would get bored if she was there all year round.

Chelsea and Sophia slid into a booth and enjoyed draft beers in chilled mugs while they waited for their food. The place felt a little rustic, with wood everywhere, and enough whiskey on the wall behind the bar to paralyze a thousand mules. If mules drank whiskey. She even liked the string of Christmas lights around the perimeter and the giant Christmas tree in the corner. Was the beer hitting her or was her mood changing about the season?

Fifteen minutes later the waiter delivered two burgers and a basket of beer-battered fries.

Sophia took a sip of her beer. "Good timing. I was feeling a little tipsy."

"Anything else I can get for you?" the waiter asked.

"I think we're good." She eyed the food, ready to dive in. "This smells so good. Thank you."

"My pleasure. Enjoy." The waiter hesitated. "By the way . . . I'm a big fan. I've seen all your movies with my children. My ten-year-old says she wants to be like you when she grows up. She's growing her hair to catch up with you."

Sophia smiled. "Thank you. I'm flattered."

The waiter walked away, which was refreshing since most people asked for an autograph or a selfie. She knew it came with the territory, but people interrupted her when she had a mouthful of food. Speaking of which, she was famished. Must have been that workout on the mountain.

Sophia had the sudden urge to check her phone for messages from Brad. She glanced over at her purse.

Chelsea cleared her throat. "Don't even think about it."

"I wasn't thinking of doing anything at all," she lied.

"Right. Eat up, would ya?"

Sophia was surprised how fast she let it go. That's because she knew deep down inside this trip was not only supposed to be fun, but therapeutic, too. Chelsea was a smart woman, she'd give her that.

Sophia relaxed a little more and then grabbed a couple of beer-battered French fries, and stuffed them in her mouth. "Okay, I admit this was a brilliant idea coming here."

Chelsea took a swig of her beer. "I know. I'm brilliant like that." She leaned in. "That waiter was delicious, wasn't he?"

"Knock it off."

"I was kidding. He's married with children." Chelsea grabbed her burger with both hands and held it a few inches in front of her mouth. "This is more important than men right now." She took a big bite of her burger and moaned.

Sophia laughed, then froze when she saw Ethan talking to someone just outside the restaurant.

Chelsea grabbed her napkin and wiped her mouth. "What?"

"Nothing." Sophia turned her attention away from the

window so Chelsea wouldn't notice Ethan and say something.

Chelsea glanced toward the window and her eyes lit up. "It's our neighbor!" She placed her napkin on the table and stood.

Sophia sat up in her seat. "What are you doing? Sit down!"

Chelsea ignored her and moved swiftly toward the window.

"Chelsea!"

Too late.

Chelsea knocked on the window and waved to Ethan. He turned and glanced at Chelsea, smiling and waving back.

Then Chelsea waved him inside.

God. What was she doing?

Sophia checked her teeth with her finger, finding a piece of onion. She stuck it back in her mouth, chewed and swallowed. Then she took a swig of her beer and fluffed her hair.

Chelsea slid back into the booth and smiled. "You need a mirror?"

"No, I do not need a mirror. Why did you invite Ethan in here? I look like hell."

Chelsea arched an eyebrow. "You look fine. And why do you care, anyway? We're taking a break from men, remember? No harm in just saying hello. Hello to a very handsome man . . ."

"I'm going to kill you when we get back. And I care because—"

"Hey," Ethan said, appearing out of nowhere and smiling at Sophia. "How did you do out there today?'

Had he heard their conversation? Oh no . . .

Sophia forced a smile. "Well, I think—"

"She surprised the heck out of me!" Chelsea cut in. "She kept up with me almost the entire time. You're a fantastic teacher."

Ethan shook his head. "Hey, I can't take the credit. She already had the natural talent. She would have been fine without my instruction although it was a pleasure." He winked at Sophia and dropped his gaze below her neck.

Oh, my God! The guy is ogling my boobs!

Ethan reached over and pulled a French fry from the front of Sophia's jacket. "Looks like this one missed your mouth." He handed the French fry to her. "Here you go."

Sophia found it difficult to speak and she felt the temperature go up. "I . . . uh . . . you can keep it."

Ethan inspected the fry and chuckled before popping it in his mouth. "Don't mind if I do. They have the best fries here." Ethan pointed to Sophia's face. "You okay? Looks like you got some sun this morning. Unless your beer is keeping you warm."

She nodded. "Probably the beer . . ."

Chelsea pointed to the space on the bench next to Sophia. "Have a seat."

She was going to kill her sister.

"Thanks, but I can't," Ethan said. "I was only on the schedule for a half-day of lessons because I'm having some friends over for dinner." He gestured to their food. "Your food is getting cold and I need to get back and prepare things. Merry Christmas."

"Merry Christmas," Sophia and Chelsea said together.

They both turned their heads and watched Ethan leave. He passed by the window, looked in, and waved goodbye.

Sophia picked up her burger. "See? What did I tell you? He has no interest in me." She took a bite, and washed it down with another swig of her beer.

Chelsea grabbed the ketchup bottle and smothered her half of the fries. "You're wrong. He complimented you on your skiing, winked at you, and then practically felt you up. Then he noticed your blushing cheeks. I'm sure my cheeks are just as red as yours, but did he mention mine? No. He barely even looked at me while he was here. He's interested in you all right."

"You don't know what you're talking about."

It didn't matter if Ethan was interested in Sophia, anyway. She wasn't going to put her heart into something that reality would tear apart when the vacation was over.

Ethan quietly opened the front door and sneaked inside

the house. He closed the door carefully behind him and listened for Bear. Nothing.

Good.

The dog sometimes couldn't hear a thing over his own snoring. Ethan hung up his jacket, knocking off the hanging leash.

Crap.

Hopefully, Bear didn't hear it.

Wishful thinking.

Ethan could hear the train coming, barreling from around the corner. "Woof!"

He waved his arms in the air at the dog, trying to get him to apply the brakes like he always did. "Easy, Bear. Easy, boy. Slow down! Slow! Down!"

Not going to happen.

Bear slammed into Ethan's legs and pushed him back into the coat rack. The jackets, parkas and hats from the coat rack all dropped to the floor and another Lick Festival began.

Ethan shook his head. "I love you, buddy, but I don't know what to do with you." He scratched Bear on the head and finally pushed him away. "Okay, okay. I need to get in the shower."

Ethan had a lot to do and wanted to get cleaned up before Mike, Violet and Uncle Al showed up. Fifteen minutes later he felt revived and fresh, ready to start the food preparation.

The menu for the evening was honey-baked ham, cheesy

garlic potato casserole, cranberry sauce, and sweet Hawaiian dinner rolls. For dessert, apple and pumpkin pies. Fortunately, Ethan only had to worry about the cheesy garlic potatoes casserole and the cranberry sauce since the honey-baked ham was pre-ordered and pre-cooked and the rest was being brought by Mike and Uncle Al. Still, this was his first time preparing the potato dish and he didn't want to mess up. He had found the recipe online a few weeks ago, and the reviews were fantastic.

Ethan put some Christmas music on the stereo and threw on his Rudolph sweatshirt. He hummed along to "Have Yourself a Merry Little Christmas" by Judy Garland and got to work.

Later that afternoon as he was just about ready to stick the casserole in the oven his cell phone rang. He leaned over and checked the caller ID on the kitchen counter. It was Uncle Al. Maybe he was running late since he should have already been there.

Ethan wiped his hands and answered the call. "Hey, what's up?"

"Sorry I'm running late," Uncle Al said. "I'm just around the corner. I was almost there and then realized I forgot the pies. Plus, I stopped and picked up wine coolers."

Ethan laughed. "You're still living in the eighties."

"One of these days I'll get you to try one."

"Yeah . . . keep trying."

"Mike and Violet there yet?"

"Not yet."

The doorbell rang.

"Woof!"

"They're here now."

"Woof!"

"Okay," said Uncle Al. "See you in a minute or so."

"Good." Ethan disconnected the call, wiped his hands, and went to the front door. Bear was already there sniffing away at the wood, trying to figure out who rang.

"It's Mike and Violet." Ethan pushed him out of the way and opened the door.

"Uncle Ethan!"

Ethan laughed and hugged Violet.

"Woof!"

Violet pulled away from Ethan to hug Bear. "Hi, Bear. I didn't forget about you."

Mike stepped in and closed the door. "Hey, man." He set a canvas shopping bag on the floor and hugged Ethan. "Merry Christmas."

"Merry Christmas."

Bear dug his nose in the bag.

"Hey!" Ethan lunged for the bag and held it above his shoulders, out of Bear's reach. "This is not for you."

Mike helped Violet with her jacket and hung it on the rack.

Ethan gestured toward the kitchen. "Come in—I don't want to mess up dinner."

Mike hung up his own jacket. "Smells great! I'm surprised Al is not here yet."

The doorbell rang.

"Woof!"

"Speak of the devil," Ethan said stopping and looking toward the door. "He called and said he was running late. Do you want to let Uncle Al in, Violet? He's probably got his hands full."

"Okay . . . Bear can help. Come on, Bear."

Bear followed Violet to the door.

Violet turned the handle slowly and pulled the door open. "You're not Uncle Al."

"You're right, I'm not. I'm Chelsea, the neighbor next door."

"Come in, Chelsea." Ethan stepped toward her, wondering where her fascinating and beautiful sister was.

Chelsea stepped inside and was immediately attacked by Bear's tongue.

"Bear! Quit basting the neighbor."

Chelsea stroked Bear along his back, laughing. "That's okay, I don't mind. He's such a beautiful boy."

Violet pointed to Bear. "He's thirty-five."

Chelsea arched an eyebrow. "Is that right? Well, he still looks young. What's your name?"

"I'm Violet."

"Nice to meet you, Violet. I *love* your name. It's beautiful."

"Thank you."

Chelsea inspected Ethan's Rudolph sweatshirt. "Cute."

He glanced down at the sweatshirt. "Thanks. It was a gift from Violet."

"Reminds me of my sister."

"Why is that?"

She shrugged, then laughed. "I don't want to bore you. I'm so sorry to interrupt."

"Don't even worry about it," Ethan said. "We're casual here and have an open-door policy. Is everything okay?"

"We have no electricity in the house. Thought maybe you could help."

"I'd be happy to. Maybe you tripped a circuit breaker. Were you using a lot of appliances when it went out?"

She shook her head. "When we got back from lunch the power was already out. We started a fire and waited for it to come back on, figuring it was just temporary. We called the owner of the house but it went to voicemail. But now it's been a few hours and we're getting worried since we need electricity to prepare the dinner."

"Of course. I've got a couple of things going on in the kitchen myself, so follow me before I burn Christmas Eve dinner. I need a minute or two and then I can help you."

"Thank you so much. By the way . . ." Chelsea gestured back to Violet. "Your daughter is just lovely."

Ethan stopped in the hallway. "Thanks, but she's not mine."

"Oh . . ."

He continued toward the kitchen. "She's my buddy Mike's daughter. He's around here somewhere. Mike?"

Mike came out of the bathroom. "Right here. Oh . . ." Mike wasn't expecting a woman to be in the house. "Hello."

"This is Chelsea. She rented the house next door."

Mike nodded and extended his hand. "The one who likes to play with bears?"

Chelsea laughed, shaking his hand. "No. That would be my sister. Nice to meet you."

"You, too. Are you joining us for dinner?"

"What? Oh, no! We have a little electrical problem and hopefully Ethan can figure it out. Then we'll be out of your hair." Chelsea threw her hand over her mouth. "Sorry."

Mike laughed and rubbed his bald head. "It's okay. I don't have a complex about it. You know how much money I save on haircuts and gel every year?"

Chelsea laughed. "That's a good attitude to have."

Violet came back in the room with Bear. The dog climbed up on his couch, sighed and plopped his head down on top of his front paws.

"Can I read to Bear, Daddy?" Violet asked.

"Of course, sweetie."

Violet grabbed a book from her shelf and sat on the floor next to Bear. A few seconds later she was reading to him.

Chelsea leaned into Mike. "That is the most precious

thing I've ever seen. Violet is just . . . lovely."

"Thank you. She's the best thing that's ever happened to me."

"Okay . . ." Ethan opened the oven to check on the ham. Happy that it wasn't burnt, he nodded and closed the oven door. "I'm just a little paranoid about the food."

Chelsea inhaled. "Smells good."

"Thanks. I would like to say I slaved away in the kitchen for hours making it, but the ham was smoked already. All I had to do was stick it in the oven and heat it up."

He pulled the potato casserole dish closer to him on the counter, opened the bag of bread crumbs and sprinkled them on top. "I need to pop this in the oven and I'm all yours."

"Thanks." She pointed to the casserole dish. "That doesn't look pre-made."

He chuckled. "That obvious?" He crossed his fingers. "I hope it turns out well." He glanced over at the ham in the oven. "Okay, I really didn't think this through and I don't want to mess anything up. I shouldn't leave all of this unattended, but I want to help you." Ethan looked over at Mike and raised an eyebrow.

"Hey, don't look at me," Mike said. "I'm an expert at mac & cheese, BLTs, and PB&Js. That's about it."

Chelsea laughed. "How about if I keep an eye on your food and you go check on our power problem?"

"Seriously?"

"Yes! It's the least I can do. Really."

Ethan eyed the oven again, hesitating.

"Please!" Chelsea said, pointing toward the door. "Go. I can handle this. I don't want to brag or anything, but people have compared me to Martha Stewart."

Mike huffed. "Hopefully they weren't talking about your looks because you're a thousand times prettier than—" Mike stared at Chelsea for a moment, and then lunged for his beer on the kitchen counter, taking a big swig. Then another.

Was he turning red?

Mike pointed toward the front of the house. "I think I hear Uncle Al. Yeah, I'm sure I hear him. I'll go check!"

Ethan chuckled. "I'll be right back." He grabbed his jacket from the rack.

"Oh, do you need to wear that?" Chelsea asked.

Ethan looked at the jacket and squished his eyebrows together. "Why?"

"It's really not *that* cold out. Plus, I was hoping you wouldn't cover that up." She pointed to his sweatshirt. "Sophia is a *big* Rudolph fan."

He looked down at his sweatshirt. "Seriously?"

"Oh, yeah."

He hung the jacket back on the rack, and winked at Chelsea. "Okay then."

Chapter Eight

Sophia warmed her hands in front of the wood-burning stove. There was no electricity, but at least the house was warm from the fire. She wondered what had happened to Chelsea, though. She shouldn't have taken so long just to go get Ethan. Were they having a party over there without her?

A pang of jealousy ran through her. Sophia pictured Chelsea sharing a drink with Ethan. Laughing and toasting . . . Why would that make her jealous?

The knock on the door startled Sophia, knocking the crazy thoughts of jealousy from her head.

She opened the door and sighed. "Why didn't you bring the key?"

It was Ethan.

Wearing a Rudolph sweatshirt just as ridiculous as hers.

She tried not to laugh.

Ethan followed her gaze, looking down at his sweatshirt. "It was a gift."

Sophia bit her lip and threw her hands up in defense. "I didn't say anything."

"Your eyes did. And I don't get why you find it amusing, Chelsea said you were a big fan."

"Oh, did she now?"

"Obviously," he answered, pointing to the sweatshirt Sophia was wearing, which also had Rudolph on the front.

Sophia looked down at her sweatshirt. "It was *also* a gift."

Ethan chuckled. "I guess it's the season to be grateful for the gifts we receive. Whether they make us feel awkward or not."

"Yeah . . ."

"And it's nice to see you have a body."

Sophia froze. "Excuse me?"

"I mean . . . of course you have a body. Everybody has a body. It's just, you normally like to cover yours up with ten layers of clothing."

She didn't know how to respond to that.

He clapped his hands. "Anyway, *you* need power."

"What happened to Chelsea?"

"She's watching my food so it doesn't burn."

"Oh."

Ethan entered the house and looked around. He smiled when he saw the red candles that were lit and the Christmas decorations. "Very nice."

Sophia shrugged. "The pushy man next door dumped a bunch of stuff on the porch and then played Doorbell Ditch."

"I have no idea what you're talking about." He grinned. "But he sounds like a nice guy."

"Not bad." She checked out his butt. "It's nice to see he's got a body like the rest of us."

One hell of a body.

Ethan turned around and she lifted her gaze.

He arched an eyebrow.

Did he catch me checking out his butt? God! Don't do that!

He looked suspicious, but then looked around the house a little more. "Okay, I need to go downstairs and check out the breaker box. Do you know if there's a flashlight around? I can go back to the house if there isn't one."

Sophia pointed to the bricks near the wood-burning stove. "Over there."

"Great. I'll be right back."

Ethan clicked on the flashlight and headed down the stairs by the side of the kitchen. She heard him making some noise down there. Was he talking to himself?

She moved closer to the stairs to listen, but his voice was muffled and she couldn't make out a word. She took the opportunity to grab a candle and look at her hair in the mirror. It was a disaster!

"What are you doing?" Sophia mumbled to herself a few minutes later after she caught herself obsessing with her hair.

"Pardon me?" Ethan said, coming back up from the lower level.

"Nothing. What did you find out?"

"You didn't trip a breaker, so I called one of my buddies

over at the power company. He said there are several hundred houses in the area without power. A truck carrying construction supplies hit a power pole, causing a transformer to blow."

"That doesn't sound good. Why do *you* have power then?"

"I have a Tesla Powerwall."

"Tesla, like the car?"

He nodded. "They also manufacture backup power supply systems for homes and businesses. I learned my lesson the hard way when I was preparing a Thanksgiving dinner a few years back and the power went out. Had to toss everything out." He stopped talking when he realized she probably didn't care about his past Thanksgivings. She needed power, not chit chat. "Sorry I couldn't help you this time."

She shrugged. "It's probably a good thing. I was beginning to think you were Superman."

Ethan grinned. "Darn—so close. Guess I need to work harder if I want to be a superhero. That could be a lot of fun."

"It can be."

He chuckled. "You were a superhero in another life?"

No. On the big screen. "I guess you could say that," Sophia answered, now realizing she was moving dangerously close to giving away too much personal information about her life in Hollywood.

"Hopefully this doesn't mess up your dinner plans for the evening."

"We'll figure something out."

"You can always join us for dinner, if you'd like."

She jerked her head back, not expecting that at all.

"I mean . . . We always have way too much food, so it's no big deal at all."

"That's all right," Sophia said. "We don't want to intrude on your Christmas Eve dinner."

"Why not?"

"Because . . . No, thanks. And hopefully I'm *not* being a bitch this time, but no thank you."

He studied her for a moment.

She avoided eye contact. "I know you're looking at me. Knock it off."

Ethan chuckled. "You're a fascinating creature, Sophia."

"Is that a compliment?"

"Oh, it's *definitely* a compliment."

She looked up and they locked eyes for a moment. It took a few seconds before she could let out a *thank you*.

Why did he have to be so good-looking? Sophia wanted to be repulsed by him! No such luck. He was a giant piece of candy for her eyes, and her sweet tooth was on high alert.

She looked away, fearing she was blushing.

Ethan smiled and turned toward the door. "Well, keep it in mind. The offer's open if you'd like to join us for dinner or dessert or a cup of cheer. And I have a second fridge downstairs if you need to bring things over to keep them cold. Just come over. Anytime."

"Thank you."

He stared at her again. "You're not coming over, are you?"

She shrugged. "No. I'm afraid not."

"Well, then. There's only one thing I can do, I guess."

"What's that?"

"I'll just have to invite Chelsea."

"No!" she said, practically jumping down his throat. "If you invite her she will pester me and pester me until I agree to go with her."

"She'd do that?"

"Yes. She's relentless and drives me crazy sometimes."

He nodded. "Okay, then . . ."

"Okay, then *what?*"

"Nothing. See you later."

"No, you won't."

He winked and left without saying another word.

God! Why did she tell him that? He was going to invite Chelsea now. He wasn't bluffing. Then she would come back and give Sophia crap until she caved in and agreed to go. No way.

She wouldn't let it happen. She would be strong when Chelsea came back and let her know there was no way in hell she was going to go over to Ethan's for dinner.

Sophia snuck over to the window and watched him walk

back to his house.

Why had she said no? And why had she been so adamant about it?

The truth was a traditional holiday dinner sounded wonderful. She couldn't remember the last time she had had one. And dinner with Ethan sounded even better. She couldn't deny the attraction considering the way her body responded when he had looked at her that way. She was sure she had seen a sparkle in his eye when he talked to her. Looked like they had some chemistry going on, for sure. Who knew what type? Like it mattered.

Sophia and Chelsea were taking a break from men.

Besides, even if she *were* interested in that tall, hunky mountain man with the firm butt, there was no way it would work out. She had her life in Hollywood. He had his life in Lake Tahoe.

She lifted her gaze as Chelsea finally came out of Ethan's house.

"Here we go," Sophia mumbled to herself. "Stay strong. Don't give in."

Chelsea stomped each foot in the snow as she got closer to the house, then she stomped up the stairs and across the deck.

Sophia moved to the living room, squared her shoulders and waited.

The door opened and then slammed shut. "Sophia!"

"No need to yell, I'm right here."

Chelsea continued her stomping, this time toward the living room. She stopped and placed her hands on her hips, ready for the showdown. "Why did you turn down dinner with Ethan?"

"Because I—"

Chelsea held her hand up. "I don't want to hear it. Put on your shoes and let's go. We're having dinner over there."

"No, we're not."

"Yes, we *are*. Now."

"We're supposed to be taking a break from—"

"Yada yada yada. Quit thinking so much. I know you got screwed over last Christmas and I know you don't trust men."

"Glad we got that cleared up."

"Look, that was the past. We don't have electricity and *I* want to have a wonderful Christmas Eve dinner. They have the best Christmas music playing over there—you'll love it. And you should see the spread! You should *smell* it! Ham, potato casserole . . ."

"Potato casserole?"

"Yes! Ethan made it and it looks divine!"

"God! He can cook too? That's just not playing fair."

"He also made cranberry sauce. Oh! For dessert they have pumpkin pie and apple—"

"Stop!" Sophia's stomach was grumbling. "You know I make bad decisions when I'm hungry. No way. I don't want to go over there."

"Why not?"

"I don't know!" she lied.

She knew the reason. Sophia knew she would enjoy Ethan's company. Probably too much. He was kind and handsome and compassionate and funny.

He was all wrong for her!

Chelsea let out a deep breath. "Well, I'm going back over there."

Sophia looked around the house and frowned. "You would seriously leave me here? All alone?"

"Yes."

"You're bluffing."

"You. Just. Watch." She turned and marched back toward the door. "See ya later!"

"Wait!'

Sophia had no intention of spending Christmas Eve by herself.

Chelsea stopped and turned back around, waiting for Sophia to say something.

"Why do you want me to go so bad?" Sophia asked.

Chelsea sighed. "Did you already forget I went through a horrible divorce? I need something like this. I deserve it, too."

Sophia couldn't argue with that. This was the first time in a long time that Chelsea looked alive. She almost looked happy! She loved seeing her sister happy and if she wanted to go next door, Sophia would just have to suck it up and go with her.

"Potato casserole, huh?"

Chelsea nodded. "You could probably have seconds, too, but you need to leave room for the apple pie."

"You know I don't need room to eat apple pie."

"True."

"Okay," Sophia mumbled.

Chelsea moved closer and cupped her ear with one hand. "What was that?"

"I said okay!"

"Yes!" Chelsea raced toward Sophia and grabbed her in a bear hug, squeezing her tight. "This will be great, you'll see. I love you, but you're the most stubborn woman I know."

"Likewise."

"And guess what? I met a guy!"

Sophia blinked. "What are you talking about?"

"He's so nice! Cute too, even with his bald head."

"Bald head? I told you I don't want you dating a bald guy!"

"Dating? Ha! I'm going to marry that guy."

Now Chelsea was talking crazy. She was gone fifteen minutes max and now she was talking about marriage?"

"Wait, wait, wait," Sophia said, trying to stop her head from spinning. "Who was the one who said she didn't want to go to Vegas because she feared she would get drunk and end up married again in an Elvis chapel?"

"I'm thinking more of a quaint garden ceremony or

something on the beach."

"You're crazy. And how could you have met a guy? You just went over to Ethan's house. Are you talking about him?"

"No! He's not my type, you know that. It's Ethan's best friend. His name is Mike, and he has the most *beautiful* daughter. Violet. They're both amazing. He's a widower which is sad but also great because he's single. I mean, if I had to choose between him being single and him getting his wife back I would want him to have his wife back, of course. But that's a moot point because he's single and I'm ready to mingle!"

"Did you drink espresso while you were over there?"

"What? No! I'm just . . . excited."

She stared at Chelsea. "So *that's* why you're so excited about dinner over there. This has nothing to do with you getting over your divorce and us having a wonderful Christmas Eve dinner with Christmas music. You've got the hots for a man already!"

"I admit meeting Mike may have influenced my decision to have dinner over there a little. Or a lot."

"So much for our break."

"Women say they want and need a break from men, but that's complete, utter crap. Deep down inside we *all* dream of another man coming into our lives. Holding us. Kissing us. Cherishing us. And plowing us!"

Sophia snorted. "You're unbelievable."

"I wanna be plowed like the Tahoe snow!"

Chapter Nine

Ethan glanced over at the front door again, waiting—hoping —for a knock or a ring. Chelsea said she would change Sophia's mind about coming over for Christmas Eve dinner.

They should be here by now.

He believed Chelsea could convince her, even if Sophia was as stubborn as a mule. He was sure her attitude had less to do with her being stubborn and independent and more to do with her being burned in the past by a guy or two. Too bad.

Sophia was growing on Ethan.

He slid on the gloves and pulled the potato casserole out of the oven, still thinking about Sophia. Maybe he'd take leftovers to them later if Chelsea weren't successful in getting her sister to change her mind. He chuckled, thinking of how Sophia would react to that!

Mike grabbed a pita chip and dipped it in the hummus. "What's so funny?"

"Nothing. Just thinking of Sophia."

Mike nodded as he chewed. "I was thinking of Chelsea. Maybe you should go back over there and try harder to get them to join us."

Ethan shook his head. "You heard Chelsea—she said she'd take care of it. It's still early and we've got a little more time before dinner's on the table, anyway." He stuck the Hawaiian dinner rolls in the oven. "If it's meant to be it's meant to be, but I must admit I would enjoy the company of those two beautiful women."

Mike held out his beer bottle toward Ethan. "I'll drink to that."

Ethan clinked his bottle. "Cheers."

"Hey, hey . . . Don't leave me out." Uncle Al clinked both of their bottles with his. "And when are you two sissies going to dive into a manly wine cooler? I brought a twelve-pack and I can't drink the whole thing by myself."

Ethan chuckled. "Isn't that an oxymoron? Manly wine cooler?"

The doorbell rang.

"Woof!"

Ethan glanced over at Mike and grinned. "Looks like Chelsea is a miracle worker."

They toasted again.

Ethan set his beer on the kitchen counter and walked to the front door.

Bear was already there, sniffing as usual.

"Okay, buddy. Out of the way, you big lug." He nudged Bear to the side with his hip and opened the door, getting the surprise he was hoping for.

Sophia and Chelsea.

"Welcome," Ethan said, opening the door farther and winking at Chelsea. "So glad you could make it."

"Thanks for having us," Chelsea said, giving Ethan a knowing smile and holding out two bags. "We brought some appetizers and a few things to stick in your refrigerator downstairs so they don't go bad."

"Of course. Thanks for the appetizers." He grabbed the two bags from her and set them off to the side. "Please come in and hang your jackets up right there."

Ethan closed the door behind Chelsea and Sophia as they hung up their jackets. Bear began his usual licking. The girls didn't seem to mind, each taking their turns petting his big boy.

Ethan turned to Sophia, trying to keep a straight face. "What made you change your mind?"

Sophia crossed her arms. "You *know* Chelsea changed my mind. You don't play fair."

"Ahhh, that's where you're wrong. I *always* play fair. I told you ahead of time I would invite Chelsea. I didn't lie."

"That *was* honest of him, don't you think?" Chelsea jumped in.

"Honest Ethan—that's me."

Sophia held out a bottle of wine for Ethan. "Here you go, Honest Ethan. Sorry we couldn't bring anything cooked, but the reason is obvious."

"I think you need a hug."

"I'm so close to kicking you."

"I would enjoy watching you try."

Chelsea laughed. "You two bicker like an old married couple."

"This wasn't necessary," Ethan said, inspecting the bottle and smiling at Sophia. "I'm just glad you came over. Christmas is better with friends and family."

Sophia smiled and nodded but didn't respond.

Holy smokes. What a smile.

Ethan's heart beat shifted into overdrive. "I heard you're a fan of potato casserole."

She nodded. "Die-hard fan."

"Good."

Chelsea and Sophia followed him into the kitchen. Uncle Al was relaxing on the recliner, looking at something on his phone. Mike was flipping through Ethan's music collection. Violet was working on a puzzle on the floor.

Ethan set the wine on the table. "Hey, everyone. Sophia and Chelsea are joining us for dinner."

Uncle Al popped up from the recliner and then froze.

Mike placed a stack of Christmas CDs back on the shelf, turning and stopping in his tracks.

It was like they both had seen a ghost.

"What happened?" asked Ethan.

Mike was staring at Sophia.

Uncle Al was staring at Sophia.

"What is this?" Ethan asked, his eyes darting back and forth between Mike and Uncle Al. "Day of the Zombies?"

Violet got up from the floor. Her scream was loud and unexpected. "Lady Karma!"

You'd probably have heard a pin drop if "A Holly Jolly Christmas" had not been playing on the stereo.

Ethan cocked his head to the side and studied Sophia. "Yeah . . . I guess she kind of looks like Lady Karma."

"She *is* Lady Karma, you idiot," Uncle Al scolded him.

Ethan turned to Sophia again. "Oh . . ." He swallowed hard. "Sophia, as in . . . Sophia Harris?"

Sophia nodded. "That would be me."

Violet approached Chelsea. "Lady Karma is your sister?"

"She sure is," Chelsea said, smiling proudly.

"Wow. You're *so* lucky."

"*That* I am."

Ethan cracked his knuckles, deep in thought. Uncle Al had called it correctly. He was an idiot. How could he not have known she was Lady Karma? One of the biggest movie stars in the world was staying next door and he'd had no clue. Everyone knew except for him!

In his defense, Ethan read a lot in his free time. He hadn't watched one movie since Lorraine slept with that actor and they had broken up. His not recognizing Lady Karma made perfect sense since she had just become popular in the last few years, when he had distanced himself from everything that had to do with Hollywood. Still, everyone was still staring at him.

He jammed his hands in his pockets and shook his head in embarrassment. "This is a little awkward."

Chelsea rubbed Ethan's shoulder and leaned in. "Don't be embarrassed. Out of seven billion people in the world, you're the only one who doesn't know who my sister is! You should get an award for that."

"Or a dunce cap." He let out a deep sigh. "Look, the truth is I don't really watch television and I haven't been to the movies in years."

"It's not a big deal," Sophia said.

Chelsea laughed. "It's cute."

"Cute . . ." Ethan set the cranberry sauce off to the side and then clapped his hands for everyone. "Okay, getting close here and I'm going to create diversions to distract everyone from my stupidity. Mike, can you do me a favor and grab the two bags in the entryway? One has appetizers and the other bag goes to the refrigerator downstairs."

"Sure thing."

"Thanks. Uncle Al, do you mind getting these two ladies a beverage of their choice while I finish up here?"

Uncle Al stepped into the kitchen and gave Ethan a look. "Why are you calling me Uncle Al? I'm George Clooney. You didn't know that either? I'm highly offended."

Chelsea and Sophia laughed.

Ethan shook his head. "Okay, I see how this evening's going to go."

"Oh, believe me. We will talk about this until your last

day on earth." Uncle Al chuckled. "Okay, ladies, we have wine, beer, or . . ." He held up his bottle and smiled. "Wine coolers!"

Chelsea laughed. "Sure, I'll have a wine cooler. Haven't had one in forever . . ."

"That sounds good," Sophia said. "Me, too."

Uncle Al winked at Ethan. "The ladies know a good thing when they see it, unlike the owner of this establishment."

Ethan pulled the ham from the oven, then glanced over at Sophia. She must have felt his gaze and looked over, locking eyes with him for a few seconds before he pulled the electric carving knife from the drawer.

Twenty minutes later the appetizers were gone and everyone was seated at the dining table, ready to eat dinner.

Ethan raised his beer for a toast. "To friends and family and special guests. Merry Christmas."

"Merry Christmas," they all said together, toasting.

Uncle Al kept his bottle raised. "One more toast . . . To those who have seen us at our best and seen us at our worst and can't tell the difference."

"Cheers," they all said together.

Sophia glanced over at Ethan and wondered what he was thinking. They hadn't spoken a word since he had found out who she was. He'd given a nice toast and smiled, but the smile never reached his eyes. Most people were excited to meet her, but now that he knew who she was he didn't seem the same.

Something was off.

She'd hate for it to get weird, but it looked like the evening was headed in that direction.

Too bad . . .

Sophia liked Ethan—she even had a crush on him, to be honest. No way she would tell Chelsea that. God, it sounded like she was in the eighth grade, but it was the truth. What was she doing? She pulled her eyes away from the gorgeous man and looked for a distraction, finding it in the corner. It was the seven-foot Noble Fir Christmas tree with the colorful string lights. It was adorned with glass ball ornaments, hanging pinecones, and topped off with a glittering mesh angel. She was surrounded by the excitement and magic of the holidays.

"All I Want For Christmas Is You" played in the background.

Not the version from Mariah Carey. The one from the movie *Love Actually*.

What was the name of the cute girl who sang it?

Sophia couldn't remember. She should remember since she had met her at a party held by the movie studio. *Hmmm.* Liam Neeson's son in the movie had had a crush on the girl.

A crush.

Sophia's mind went back to Ethan.

She picked up her wine cooler and studied the bottle. What was in that thing?

Focus!

Now she felt like giggling.

That's what happened when she wasn't stressed out. She had had a lot on her mind the last few months, but not now. At the moment she felt normal and relaxed. What a difference a few days made. It wasn't that long ago when she wanted a hitman for Christmas to kill all the A-list actresses in Hollywood. Now all she needed was another serving of the potato casserole and she'd be the happiest girl in the world.

She chuckled at the thought.

Uncle Al pointed to Sophia's face. "What was that laugh for?"

Sophia shrugged. "I was just thinking how Chelsea and I ended up here tonight with all of you and it wasn't even planned."

"Sometimes the best plans are no plans at all," he said holding up his wine cooler to toast her.

"I agree," she replied, clinking his bottle. "This is wonderful. Thank you. Thank you all."

Ethan was still quiet.

"It's a pleasure to have you here," Mike said. "If you don't mind me asking, how do you normally celebrate Christmas Eve?"

"Well . . ." Sophia shrugged. "Normally . . . I don't."

Everyone at the table stopped talking and turned to Sophia.

"You don't believe in Santa?" Violet asked, a frown forming on her face.

"Of course she does," Chelsea jumped in to the rescue. "It's just she gets so busy making movies—especially when she has to travel. It's so much more than you see on the big screen. There are meetings, and make-up, and running through lines. Long, long days."

"Oh, believe me, I know," Violet said, without missing a beat.

Sophia turned to Violet. "Have you been on a movie set?"

Violet shook her head. "Not yet. I prefer the theater."

Sophia smiled. "I *love* the theater. I started my career on Broadway, so it will always have a special place in my heart. What have you seen?"

Mike cleared his throat. "Actually, Violet has done some acting, too. Obviously nothing on Broadway, but we have a well-known conservatory theater here in Tahoe and she's been part of the program for the last two years."

"That's wonderful! What have you been in?"

Violet used her fingers to count. "*Pippi Longstocking. The Lion, The Witch, and the Wardrobe.* And *Cinderella.* Tomorrow we have our last performance of *A Charlie Brown Christmas.*"

"My favorite! But I'm surprised because even I don't

have to work on Christmas Day. Will people show up?"

"We hope so," Mike answered. "It's a fundraiser."

"I play Lucy," Violet said. "She's not an easy character because she's crabby and bossy and it's hard for me to be mean. I wanted the role of Sally, Charlie Brown's younger sister, but they gave the part to Madison Lee."

Sophia nodded and took a long swig of her wine cooler. "I know *exactly* how you feel. It's like a slap in the face when they give a part you desperately wanted to someone else. It's not fair—especially when you know you can play the part just as well as they can or even better. The producers and the director don't always know what's best, but they should have *the gonads* to take a chance on a person now and then, you know? Especially when that person has a proven track record!" Sophia drained the rest of her wine cooler and set the bottle back down on the table. "That really sucks."

Everyone stared at Sophia. Again.

Awkward. Round two.

"Your face is red," Violet said. "Are you okay?"

Sophia nodded and forced a smile. "I'm fine—thanks. I guess I got a little carried away."

"That's okay. Madison is my best friend, so I shouldn't be mad she got the part. Dad says I should be happy because we both got parts. Anyway, I get carried away too sometimes, but Dad usually tells me I'm not acting my age, so I stop." She stared at Sophia. "What are gonads?"

Uncle Al smirked. "Ask your grandmother."

Chapter Ten

Snap out of it!

Ethan didn't like his current state of mind and he knew it had everything to do with his ex, Lorraine. All those negative thoughts about Hollywood—the materialistic, selfish, egotistical, cheating lifestyle—came pouring right back in when he found out Sophia was mega movie star Sophia Harris. He felt differently about her now.

Ethan didn't want to lump everyone in Hollywood in the same category, but this was one part of his brain he was having a tough time controlling. He needed to get those thoughts out of his head because he didn't want to spend Christmas Eve in a downer mood.

He took a sip of his beer, not paying too much attention to the conversation Sophia was having with Violet about acting.

What had happened to Sophia? It sounded like she didn't get a certain role she wanted, which made little sense at all. Shouldn't the biggest movie star in the world be able to pick whatever role she wanted? Wouldn't they be knocking down her door with offers every single day?

Now he knew why random people had said hello to

Sophia on the slopes. And why she acted so weird and covered her face with her hair sometimes when she was in public. Mummy Woman was doing her best to hide who she was.

Uncle Al waved a hand in front of Ethan's face. "Is my nephew drunk?"

Ethan sat up in his chair. "I've only had one beer so far." He glanced around the table; all eyes were on him. He must have missed what they were talking about.

"Well, then?" asked Uncle Al.

He shrugged. "Well what?"

"*Answer* the question. If you could make one Christmas wish right now you know would come true, what would it be?"

Ethan looked across the table at Violet who was sitting on the edge of her seat like she was waiting for an answer.

"World peace?"

Uncle Al slapped Ethan on the back. "Jesus, this isn't a Miss America pageant. Give us something good."

Ethan shrugged. "World peace is good."

"I know it's good, but everyone says that. At least Sophia was keeping it real and said she wanted an Academy Award."

God, how much of the conversation did I miss? And what kind of wish is that? An Academy Award? Out of all the possible things in the world?

Maybe Sophia already had everything she needed.

"Earth to Ethan, we need an answer. You're not supposed to think about it so much. Just say the first thing that pops into your head. What do you wish for? Go!"

"More snow," Ethan answered, which was the truth.

Just about everyone Ethan knew hoped for more snow. A couple of big storms was all they needed for the businesses in the valley to have a bountiful season. And that meant the tourists would be happy.

"Good one!" Uncle Al said, grabbing Ethan's arm and squeezing it. "I wish for more snow, too! Mike? What's your wish?"

Mike reached over and tugged gently on Violet's ear. "I'd like to give my wish to Violet so she gets *two* wishes."

"You can't do that, Dad."

Mike laughed along with everyone else. "Fine. I'll stick with the guys. I wish for more snow, too."

"Finally!" Uncle Al said. "Chelsea?" What about you?"

She rubbed her chin and glanced over toward the kitchen. "I'm going to have to say my wish is for . . . Christmas cookies."

Uncle Al pointed to the kitchen. "The apple and pumpkin pies over there are *not* going to be thrilled with your wish. Twenty-nine percent of Americans prefer *pie* after their holiday meals. Only fifteen percent prefer cookies."

"Well, I guess I'm in the minority then."

Mike cocked his head to the side. "That's all you wish for? Cookies?"

"*Christmas* cookies. And yeah, that's all . . . For me life is about the simple things. I'm a Christmas cookie kind of girl."

"I'm a Christmas cookie kind of guy."

Chelsea smiled. "Well then, I guess *you* need to change your wish from snow to cookies."

Mike raised a hand in the air. "I wish for Christmas cookies."

Holy crap.

Something was happening between Mike and Chelsea. Ethan was sure of it.

"Chelsea just may be in luck. Isn't that right, sweetie?" Mike winked at Violet, who jumped up from her seat and practically sprinted to the kitchen.

"Woof!"

Bear jumped off his couch and followed Violet.

"Bear!" Ethan called out. "You know you can't eat sugar. Back on your couch."

Bear leaned over his water bowl, took a couple of slurps with his giant tongue, then turned around and dripped all the way back to his couch.

Violet pulled the plastic away from the large red plate on the counter, removed a cookie, and returned to the table with it. She handed the cookie to Chelsea. "I made them this morning."

Chelsea's eyes grew wide. "You did? Well then, I *definitely* have to try them. Thank you." She took a bite and moaned. "These are so good!"

"Thanks."

"They look fantastic." Uncle Al raised his hand. "Forget the snow, I wish for a cookie, too."

Violet smiled proudly and went to the kitchen to grab more cookies, quickly returning to give one to Uncle Al and the other to her dad.

Ethan stood and grabbed a stack of plates. "I want to try the cookies too, but I'll make coffee first and bring the pies over."

Uncle Al pointed to Violet with his cookie. "Wait! Violet needs to make a wish."

"That's right." Ethan sat back down and waited for her wish.

"My wish is to raise enough money to keep the theater open," Violet said.

Mike moved closer and kissed his daughter on the cheek. "Good wish, sweetie."

"What's going on with the theater?" Sophia asked.

"Well . . ." Mike said. "The theater and all of its conservatory programs are non-profit. Donations dried up after the big fire and the drought just made everything worse. We had several grants from the local government and those are going away in the new year, too. Lots of changes, but we're still hopeful."

Sophia frowned. "That's too bad."

"That's why we have an extra Christmas day performance tomorrow. It's a fundraiser."

"Are tickets still available?" asked Chelsea.

Mike nodded. "Yes." He glanced back and forth between Chelsea and Sophia. "Are you interested in going?"

Violet sat up in her seat. "Please come!"

Ethan cleared his throat. "I'm sure they've already got plans, so—"

"We would love to," Sophia said, cutting off Ethan.

He could have sworn she gave him a look. What was that all about? It was like she said yes just to stick it in Ethan's face. Was he overanalyzing this?

"Yes!" Violet hugged Chelsea, then ran around to hug Sophia.

Ethan stood again and grabbed a few more things from the table. "Okay, time to make coffee." He stuck the plates in the sink and pulled out the bag of ground coffee and container of sugar.

Violet pulled Chelsea and Sophia toward the Christmas tree and showed them her favorite ornaments while Uncle Al slid into the recliner to get comfortable. If it was like any past Christmases, he would be asleep in no time.

Ethan scooped coffee into the filter and slid it back in the machine.

Mike entered the kitchen but didn't say a word.

Ethan glanced over Mike's shoulder at the girls to make sure they weren't looking, then held his palm up in front of Mike's face. "Don't say it."

"Don't say what?"

"I know that look on your face."

"Of course you do. That's the look that tells you you're acting odd. Don't be embarrassed just because you've had one of the biggest movie stars on the planet under your nose and didn't even know it. It could happen to just about . . ." He smirked. "Nobody!" Mike laughed and nudged Ethan on the side of his arm. "Just you!"

"Keep it down."

Mike looked back. "Relax. They're all talking, plus the music is going. They can't hear a thing. So, what's going on? Why were you so quiet over dinner?"

"You *know* why."

"Lorraine?"

"The one and only."

"What does that have to do with Sophia?"

"It has plenty to do with her. Lorraine cheated on me with *an actor*." He gestured to Sophia with his eyebrows. "*She's* an actor. This is all connected."

"First of all, she's an actress, not an actor."

"You know what I mean."

"Hang on . . . We're not finished here." Mike walked around the kitchen island, grabbed a few more plates from the table and returned to the kitchen, placing them in the sink. "So Lorraine cheated on you with an actor, and you think *all* actors are like that? Like everyone you see in the tabloids?"

Ethan didn't answer.

"Let me ask you one simple question . . ." Mike leaned in. "Do you like her?"

Ethan jerked his head back. "What kind of question is that? I just *met* her a few days ago."

"Yeah, well, that really doesn't matter. I just met Chelsea and let me tell you, that woman is *amazing*. It's all about chemistry. Do you feel any chemistry with Sophia?"

He did, but Mike didn't have to know about that.

"Ethan? Answer me."

Ethan opened the dishwasher and blew out a deep breath. "She's on vacation and will be going home soon, hundreds of miles from here."

"Do you like her?"

"She's a stubborn woman."

"Do. You. Like. Her?"

"Yes!" Ethan yelled, prompting everyone in the house to turn in his direction.

Think of something.

"Sorry," he said, forcing a smile. He tried to think of a good lie. "Uncle Al got me excited about pie. Coming right up as soon as the coffee is ready!"

Sophia raised an eyebrow and then turned back toward the Christmas tree.

Ethan caught himself checking out her beautiful figure, but then got his focus back on Mike after feeling his best friend's stare.

"Ethan?"

"Yes. I like her, but now I have conflicted feelings since I know who she is."

Mike nodded. "Forget about who she is. It doesn't matter what she does for a living or how the public sees her. That's just a job. Think about the woman in her pure form."

Ethan stuck a couple of plates in the dishwasher. "You lost me there."

"I mean strip away the titles, the generalizations and the preconceived notions and get down to the essence of who she really is."

"Should I lie down for this?"

"I'm being serious. I'm trying to help."

He stared at Mike. The man drove a snow plow, but he sounded like Sigmund Freud.

"Fine. Go on."

"Okay . . ." Mike gestured behind him. "Look at Sophia."

Ethan glanced over Mike's shoulder again. "Okay."

"Not literally. Don't look at her in a physical sense. Look at her *mentally*. Like the image of her as a whole. What do you see?"

Ethan stared at Sophia and frowned. "A stubborn woman."

"And?"

"She's drop-dead gorgeous."

"Not physical."

"Right."

Ethan couldn't just dismiss that. She was the most beautiful woman he'd ever seen.

"Focus and tell me."

"Fine." Ethan closed his eyes for a moment and then opened them, nodding. "Okay. She has a soft, sweet side when she lets her guard down. She's a good person—I can tell. She has a fun personality, also only when she lets her guard down." He nodded. "She seems to have her guard up a lot."

"Not a surprise—look who she is. The woman is worth millions and has crazy fans all over the world. She has to be careful, don't you think? There are plenty of loser men who would take advantage of a woman like that."

Ethan pulled out the vanilla ice cream from the freezer and placed it on the counter. "I would cherish a woman like that."

"And that's my point. You're not giving it a chance. You're sabotaging any possibility of something happening between you two."

Ethan snorted. "You seriously think a woman like that would be interested in me?"

"If you pull your head out of your butt—yes!"

"Thanks a lot."

"I'm serious. You're the nicest guy I know, and you deserve the best."

Ethan glanced over at Sophia. "You're saying *she's* the best?"

He shook his head. "I'm saying she *could* be. Who knows? What I'm saying is . . . don't let your past dictate your future." He pointed to the carton of ice cream. "Vanilla has always been your favorite ice cream, right?"

Ethan nodded. "Always."

"How do you know pistachio is not just as good or even better?"

"I love pistachio."

"You know what I mean. There are *many* other incredible flavors in the world, but you've got to try them to find out."

"You never tire of metaphors, do you?"

Mike smirked. "You're a regular Einstein."

He knew his best friend was right. This was one of Ethan's favorite nights of the year and he was sabotaging it. What the hell was he doing?

Get over yourself and forget about Lorraine.

"Thanks," Ethan said, pulling coffee cups from the cupboard. "I'm not going to sabotage this."

Mike grinned. "That's what I wanted to hear."

"Woof! Woof!"

"Uncle Ethan," Violet said. "Bear has to go pee."

Chelsea turned to Violet. "How do you know?"

She gestured to Ethan. "Uncle Ethan trained him to let us know. One bark is when he wants to complain about something. Two barks is for pee. Three barks is for poop."

"You can train a dog to do that?"

Ethan shrugged. "It wasn't easy."

Mike laughed. "Violet, sweetie, let's take Bear out so he can do his business. I can bring in more firewood, too."

"I'll come too," Chelsea said. "I'd like to get some fresh air."

"Great!" Mike said.

Ethan pulled a small carton of creamer from the refrigerator. "The coffee's almost done. I need to get the pies ready and find the whipped cream, then I think we should be ready for dessert."

"Sophia, you can help him with that, can't you?" asked Chelsea.

Sophia hesitated. "Um . . . Of course."

And just like that, Ethan was in the kitchen.

Alone with Sophia.

Chapter Eleven

Sophia wondered if Chelsea could have been any more obvious. Ethan must have seen right through that set-up. She crossed her fingers that maybe he was distracted with the dessert and coffee because that was just a pathetic attempt at trying to get Sophia and Ethan alone.

Sophia, you can help him with that, can't you?

It's not like Sophia didn't want to help. She was just getting ready to offer when her sister opened her big mouth. Hopefully, it sounded sincere and not out of obligation.

"How can I help?" she asked.

"Honestly, there isn't much to do." Ethan glanced around the kitchen. "Oh, actually, I've got something. You can take the pies out of the boxes if you don't mind."

"I don't mind at all. Where do you want them? On the table?"

"That would be perfect."

"Okay then . . ." Sophia first pulled the pumpkin pie from the box and jammed her thumb right into it. She paused for a moment, made sure Ethan wasn't looking, then licked her thumb clean. After she placed the pie in the center of the table, she went back for the second one.

"You know I saw that, right?" Ethan said, chuckling and opening the refrigerator. "You're just like a kid."

Sophia waited for him to turn around and then said, "I guess you're referring to me *accidentally* getting some pie on my finger."

He chuckled again. "Accidentally . . ."

"Yes! And how did you see that if your back was to me?"

Ethan pointed to the kitchen window behind the sink and waved to her in the reflection of the glass. "It really wasn't that difficult."

"You were spying on me?"

"I admit I may have taken a peek . . . or two."

Sophia laughed. "I guess I need to watch out for you."

"I guess you do."

She pulled the apple pie out of the box, careful not to jam her finger in that one, then placed it on the center of the table next to the pumpkin pie. "No accidental finger jamming this time."

His back was turned again. "I know."

"Of course you do. Well, can you tell me where you want me to stick these?"

Ethan swung around and glanced at the two empty pie boxes. "No, I will *not* tell you where to stick them. But if it makes you feel better, you can tell *me* where to stick them."

"Tempting . . ." She laughed and placed the empty boxes on the kitchen island and walked around to the other side, closer to Ethan. "It's nice to see you smile."

"I was just about to say the same thing about you."

"I smile!"

"Not in Lake Tahoe, you don't."

"Look . . ." Sophia gave him the most exaggerated smile she could muster. "See?"

He nodded. "Very impressive. By the way, it's a pleasure to have you and Chelsea here with us this evening."

That was sweet, and it even sounded sincere.

"Thank you. You've gone out of your way for complete strangers."

He shrugged. "I would do it for anyone, really."

"I believe that . . ."

They held each other's gazes momentarily, until Uncle Al's snoring made them both jump. It was loud and clear, easily heard over the Frank Sinatra Christmas song playing on the stereo.

Sophia snorted and threw her hand over her mouth.

Ethan laughed. "You sound like him."

She snorted again, then laughed. "Sorry, I shouldn't laugh at him."

Ethan laughed with her. "Don't feel guilty—we laugh at him all the time, no big deal." He removed the safety seal from the top of the whipped cream dispenser. "So, what are your plans while you're here? More skiing, I hope?"

She nodded. "At least one more day, for sure. Then Chelsea says we should take the gondola up to the top of the mountain."

He nodded. "That's a must. It's beautiful up there. Anything else?"

"I'm not sure yet. Something you recommend?"

"Admittedly, there are few options, since just about everything in the winter has to do with snow, either skiing or snowshoeing. In the summer we've got hiking, biking, fishing, golfing, zip lining, rock climbing, and tons of things to do in and around the lake."

"Sounds like a lot of fun."

"It is. Do you ice skate?"

"I *love* to ice skate, but I don't get to do things like that often."

"Too busy?"

"No, it's just . . . well, you know, public places draw crowds and—"

"You're shy." His bottom lip quivered and then he burst in laughter.

She smacked him on the arm. "You're not very nice."

"Maybe not, but at least you think I'm Superman."

"No, I said I was beginning to *think* you were Superman. I didn't say you *were* Superman."

"Just a technicality—I'm going to keep my superhero status. But I get it—celebrities attract crowds and that can get a little crazy, right?"

She smiled. "Sometimes . . . yeah."

"Lake Tahoe's not like that. You can relax here. Be yourself."

Wouldn't that be nice?

It sounded too good to be true.

They locked eyes for a moment, and then she looked away.

"You're being shy again."

She turned back to face him. "You're going to get it."

They shared a laugh as he pulled out two knives to cut the pies.

At least the awkwardness from dinner was gone. Whatever was on Ethan's mind earlier had disappeared and that was a good thing. She loved the man's smile.

Ethan glanced down at Sophia's sweatshirt and grinned, looking like he was on the verge of laughter.

"What?" she asked

"Nothing."

There it was. He laughed again.

"Are you laughing at my sweatshirt again?"

"*You* were laughing at *my* sweatshirt. It wasn't the other way around—at least that's how I remember it."

She glanced at Rudolph on his chest and laughed.

He pointed to her face. "See? That's what I'm talking about." He winked at her as the front door open. He pulled a stack of spoons from the drawer and placed them next to the sugar.

"Woof!"

"Oh, God."

"What?" asked Sophia.

"Get behind me if you want to live."

Bear came barreling around the corner into the kitchen and charged Ethan.

He waved his arms in the air at the dog, trying to get him to apply the brakes just like all the other times. "Easy, Bear. Easy, boy. Slow down! Slow! Down!"

He slammed into Ethan's legs and mid-section, but instead of pushing him into the coat rack like he normally did in the entryway, Ethan flew into Sophia.

She wrapped her arms around Ethan's waist for stability and held on tight to try to keep from falling over, but the momentum sent them both down toward the kitchen floor.

Ethan tried to grab onto the counter, but ended up twisting around and landing directly on top of Sophia.

Bear went to work licking the side of his face.

"Stop it, Bear!"

Sophia laughed uncontrollably as a few errant licks connected with the side of her face as well. "Oh, my God! Attack of the killer tongue!"

The last thing she expected on Christmas Eve was to be pinned down by a gorgeous man and his oversized dog on a kitchen floor in Lake Tahoe. If she had a diary, this would go in it for sure.

Sophia continued to laugh, being the recipient of more than a few licks that were intended for Ethan. The dog looked even bigger from the floor as he got his focus back on Ethan's face.

"Bear. Get to your bed!" Ethan turned his head away from the onslaught of dog licks and accidentally brushed his lips against Sophia's.

Funny how that shut her up.

They both froze.

This wasn't a laughing matter any longer.

Sophia's gaze dropped to Ethan's lips and her heart rate picked up.

Ethan stared down at her, looking just as surprised.

"Uncle Ethan!" said Violet, entering the kitchen. "What are doing on top of Sophia?"

"Wow!" said Mike, walking in behind Violet. "What did we interrupt here? Violet, close your eyes, sweetie."

"I've seen adults make-out before, Dad."

"We're *not* making out," Ethan and Sophia responded together.

"Could have fooled us!" Chelsea laughed. "We can't leave you two alone for even a minute."

Sophia looked up into Ethan's eyes, then patted him on his firm chest, "You can probably get off me now."

"Yeah . . ." Ethan said, pushing himself up with his palms and then extending a hand down to Sophia to help her up.

"Thank you," she said, letting go of his hand and pulling down her Rudolph sweatshirt.

He straightened out his Rudolph sweatshirt. "Of course."

"Oh, wow!" Chelsea said, pointing at their sweatshirts. "Don't move, you two."

Ethan turned to Sophia and shrugged.

Chelsea pulled her phone from her purse. "This is just too cute." She waved her hand at Sophia. "Okay, move closer to Ethan. I *have to* have a picture."

Sophia didn't say a thing and inched closer to him.

"Closer! This will be such a cute photo."

Sophia hesitated.

"Sophia!"

To Sophia's surprise, Ethan hooked her by the shoulder and pulled her in tight up against his chest, grinning. "There you go being shy again. You'll never get anywhere in Hollywood if you don't loosen up."

Sophia reached behind and pinched Ethan on the side of his rib cage.

"Ouch!"

"Got it!" said Chelsea, checking the photo and nodding. "Oh yeah. This is a keeper."

"That's it?" asked Ethan. "What kind of picture was that? I must look like a lunatic."

Chelsea waved him off. "We can take more later." She gave Sophia a big smile and then set her phone down.

Ethan cleared his throat. "Okay, then . . . who's ready for dessert?"

Apparently, everyone was.

They all sat around the table, sipping on coffee and

eating way too much pie and ice cream. They talked about their favorite things about Christmas and their favorite foods. Sophia had to admit the evening had turned out much differently than from what she had expected, and she wouldn't have changed a thing.

"I think I'm ready for more pumpkin pie," Uncle Al said, cutting another slice and placing it on his plate. He turned to Sophia. "What are your plans for the rest of the holidays? Anything exciting?"

Sophia wiped her mouth and smiled. "Ethan asked me the same question. Well, of course, we're looking forward to seeing Violet onstage tomorrow."

Violet gave a big smile. "I can't believe you're coming."

"I wouldn't miss it for the world."

"Don't forget to take the gondola up the mountain," Uncle Al said. "Get off at the observation deck because it has better views of the valley and the lake than if you continued all the way to the top. I know that sounds weird, but trust me on that one."

"Sounds great."

He took a sip of water and held up his glass. "Did you know Lake Tahoe has enough water to supply each person in the US with fifty gallons per day for five years?"

Chelsea raised her eyebrows. "That's impossible."

Mike laughed. "*You* just opened up the flood gates. Let the statistics begin."

Uncle Al gestured to Mike. "Don't listen to him.

Anyway, I wasn't kidding. Lake Tahoe is the second deepest lake in the country. It's so deep you could stand the Empire State building in it and not see the top."

"That's amazing."

Uncle Al huffed. "That's nothing." He pointed to the water in his glass. "Lake Tahoe's water is 99.994 percent pure, making it one of the purest large lakes in the world. If you want to compare that, commercially distilled water is 99.998 percent pure."

"You'll be tested on this later," Ethan said.

Uncle Al chuckled. "I can get a little carried away sometimes, that's for sure. I think that's my cue to get comfy on the recliner again."

It only took a few minutes before Uncle Al was snoring again.

Violet giggled.

Ethan grinned and leaned into Violet. "Want to see if we can get Bear to lick his face?"

Violet lit up and whispered, "Yeah!"

It was obvious Ethan was good with kids. She was curious why such a kind, good-looking man wasn't married with children of his own. There had to be a story there.

Ethan stood and waved for everyone to follow. "Come on, let's go. Quietly."

Violet, Mike, Chelsea, and Sophia all got up from the dining table and followed Ethan to the family room.

Bear had returned to his couch earlier and was also

asleep. As Ethan approached, Bear opened one eye and then the other.

Ethan scratched the dog on the head and whispered, "Come on, Bear. Bring your saliva with you."

Violet covered her mouth, trying not to laugh as Bear got up and followed Ethan.

Ethan and Bear moved to the side of the recliner where Uncle Al's head was hanging.

An easy target for Bear.

Ethan stuck his finger close to the side of Uncle Al's face and whispered to the dog. "Bear. Lick."

Bear moved forward toward Ethan's finger.

Ethan pulled his finger away at the last second and the dog licked the side of Uncle Al's face.

Violet laughed, along with everyone else.

Uncle Al jumped in the chair and felt his face. "That's disgusting!" He used his shirt sleeve to wipe the slobber. "And *not* funny."

Violet jumped up and down, clapping her hands together. "That was fun! Let's do it again. Go back to sleep, Uncle Al."

"Not a chance. I'm going to stay awake for the next twenty years."

"Bear thinks you're tasty," Ethan said, laughing along with Violet.

"Right." He wiped his face again and grimaced. "Payback's a—" Uncle Al cut himself off when he saw Violet glance over at him. "Payback's a . . . bear." The dog looked up. Uncle Al stood and gestured toward the spare bedroom. "Okay, maybe I *will* hit the hay, but not in this room. Mind if I stay the night? Probably best if I don't drive."

Ethan smiled. "You never have to ask. That's what the extra beds are for."

Uncle Al gave everyone hugs and a kiss on the cheek to Violet before heading down the hallway.

"We should head out," Mike said, placing the palm of his hand on top of Violet's head. "My princess needs to get a good night's sleep for Santa in the morning. Plus, she has tomorrow's performance."

They said goodbye and Mike whispered something to Chelsea before he stepped outside.

Chelsea smiled. "I'd like that."

Odd. What was that all about? She'd like what?

Violet waved one last time. "See you tomorrow."

Ethan turned to Sophia and Chelsea. "And you two? Care for more coffee and pie and ice cream?"

"It's late, so we should head back," Chelsea said. "*You* have been the most gracious host. Thank you for a wonderful Christmas Eve. It was perfect." She smiled and hugged Ethan.

"It was my pleasure," Ethan said.

He turned to face Sophia, with a huge smile.

Oh no. Why is he looking at me that way?

Did Ethan expect a hug from Sophia just because

Chelsea hugged him? She was sure she would look like a cold, heartless bitch if she didn't hug him.

Just do it. And try not to enjoy it, like when he was on top of you on the kitchen floor.

"Thanks for everything," Sophia said, stepping forward quickly to hug him and get it over with. She lifted her arms and—

"Oh, God!" Sophia said, mortified. "Are you okay?"

She'd just smacked Ethan in the chin with her knuckles.

Hard.

Ethan nodded and rubbed his chin. "I'll be okay. Really."

"I'm *so* sorry." She reached up and felt the side of his face, like a doctor checking for damage. "I didn't mean to do that."

Ethan chuckled. "That's good to know. I'd hate to see the damage if you tried."

His face had just the tiniest bit of stubble. She loved how it felt under her fingers and wondered how it would feel against her neck.

Oh, God.

Ethan stopped laughing when he noticed Sophia was still rubbing the side of his face.

What the hell am I doing?

She retracted her hand quickly like he was a snapping turtle and her fingers were in danger.

"Maybe you should kiss it and make it better," Chelsea

blurted out.

Sophia twisted toward her sister. "How old are you?" She turned back to Ethan. "Don't mind my sister, she's a little crazy in the head."

Chelsea pointed up toward the top of the door frame. "You're standing under mistletoe, that's what I meant. It's normal to kiss. Expected, even."

Both Ethan and Sophia looked up. Sure enough, they were standing under mistletoe.

"Did you stick that there?" Sophia asked, putting on her jacket.

Ethan shook his head. "Uncle Al did. He said it promotes good health because kissing lowers your blood pressure by 3.65 percent."

Chelsea slipped on her jacket and smirked. "Well, don't you want to have lower blood pressure?"

Ethan hesitated with his answer, glancing over at Sophia first before responding. "My blood pressure is fine."

"Mine, too!" Sophia practically yelled. "Okay, then . . ." Sophia broke eye contact with Ethan and yanked her sister out the door by the arm. "Thanks again!" She was already halfway down the stairs.

"What about your things in the refrigerator downstairs?" he called out.

"Tomorrow!" Sophia yelled back.

She dragged Chelsea across the snow, up the stairs of their rental, and inside. Then she closed the door behind them and leaned back against the door, letting out a deep sigh.

"What is wrong with you?" Chelsea asked.

Sophia pointed to the lights. "Hey, the power is back on!"

"Don't try to change the subject. You like Ethan, don't you?"

Sophia didn't answer because it was true. Maybe Ethan wasn't like all the other men she had dated. Definitely not like the men in Hollywood.

Yup.

She liked him all right.

No doubt about it.

"Sophia? Talk to me."

Sophia didn't want to talk about it, but she knew Chelsea would keep pestering her. "If you must know, I am fascinated by the man. A little."

"Fascinated? Ha! I know it's more than that."

"Let's talk about something else, like you and Mike. You both seem to be getting chummy."

Chelsea's eyes grew wide. "Oh, wow. Unlike you, I'm bold enough to admit I like him a lot. He owns two businesses. Did you know that? Of course you don't know. He clears snow during the winter, has contracts with many people driving one of those snow plows. Remember when I told you I wanted to be plowed? Ha! *That* is a sign!"

Sophia couldn't help but laugh at that one. "You're too

funny."

"Seriously, he's a family man, has a stable life, and is just a good person overall."

Sophia placed a couple of pieces of wood in the wood-burning stove, then balled up some newspapers and stuck them underneath before lighting it. "But he lives here and *you* live in Beverly Hills."

"So what? Things always have a way of working out. If it's meant to be it's meant to be."

Sophia nodded. "What did he whisper to you before he left?"

Chelsea smiled. "He asked if I wanted to join him and Violet for snowshoeing after the theater. Of course I said yes." She grabbed Sophia's hands. "Oh, I hope you don't mind. It most likely won't be that long and—"

"Don't worry about it. I'm a big girl. I can just catch up on my reading or—"

"Or you can do something with Ethan!"

"I'm sure he's working and would you quit trying to make something happen between us?"

"As long as you promise not to prevent something from happening between you. I see some serious potential there."

"You need glasses."

Chapter Twelve

Sophia propped herself up on her elbows in bed the next morning after she heard the bloodcurdling scream from her sister in the other room. Chelsea was inside the house, so it couldn't have anything to do with a bear. So what was it?

It had better be good because Sophia was having the most amazing dream and Ethan was in it. He was holding her in his arms in the snow.

"No way!" Chelsea yelled again from the other room.

Sophia quickly slid out of the bed and into her slippers, hoping Chelsea was okay. Maybe something was really wrong.

"It's soooo beautiful!" Chelsea added.

Sophia let out a sigh of relief. Whatever it was, it obviously wasn't life-threatening. She glanced back at the clock.

8:00 a.m.

Not a bad night's sleep, even though she would have preferred to continue that dream.

Sophia opened her bedroom door and walked down the hallway, looking around. "Where are you?"

"In the living room!"

Sophia made her way toward the living room, wiping her eyes along the way.

It was great to have electricity again. Chelsea had already plugged in the lights of the Christmas tree and had a fire going. It looked festive. Smelled festive. Chelsea must have been motivated to start the fire on her own.

And then Sophia realized something.

"It's Christmas!" Sophia said, surprised she had forgotten.

"Duh!" Chelsea said. "Of course it's Christmas, silly. Typically it's the day after Christmas Eve. Don't ask me why." She smiled and spread her welcoming arms to Sophia, giving her a big hug. "Merry Christmas."

"Merry Christmas." She pushed away from Chelsea, curious. "Why the hell were you screaming? You interrupted a *very* nice dream."

"I was screaming . . ." Chelsea grabbed Sophia by the hand and pulled her to the window. "Because of this!"

Sophia inched up closer to the glass and her mouth dropped open.

It was snowing.

Snowing on Christmas day.

Sophia just stared as thousands of snowflakes drifted toward the ground, floating almost, like they weren't in a hurry to get there.

Sophia smiled. "It's beautiful. Magical . . ."

"It is."

The path that was carved in the snow to Ethan's house yesterday had all but disappeared, leaving nothing but a smooth, untouched area of virgin powder that reminded Sophia of the wonderful dream she'd just woken up from.

In the dream Ethan had kissed Sophia in the snow, just like Mr. Darcy had kissed Bridget at the end of the movie *Bridget Jones's Diary*. And the same song was playing, "Someone Like You" by Van Morrison. It was one of the best dreams she'd had in a long time.

So romantic.

Of course, they weren't in England in Sophia's dream and Sophia was wearing more than just underwear. Ethan was much more good-looking than Mr. Darcy, too—which was saying a lot because Sophia thought Colin Firth was very handsome in that movie.

She had always wanted to be kissed in the snow. Sophia was known for her action movies, but she was a romantic at heart. She smiled at the thought of that kiss.

"That looks like a happy grin if I've ever seen one," Chelsea said. "What are *you* thinking about?"

"Don't make a big deal out of it, but I was thinking of Ethan."

Chelsea wrapped her arms around her sister and squeezed her tight. "Looks like you're loosening up. That's good. I told you this trip was a good idea."

Sophia nodded. "You're *such* a wise woman."

"I agree!"

Ethan appeared in the window and looked over to Sophia, raising a hand and smiling.

Sophia waved back.

Then Chelsea giggled.

Sophia turned to her. "What?"

"Nothing."

"Tell me."

"Okay." She glanced down at Sophia's pajamas. "He can see what you're wearing."

Oh, God.

She was wearing her pajamas. Her bright red pajamas with the top that said "Santa's Little Helper" right across the chest in big white letters.

Last night she was displaying her support for Rudolph, now she was making it well-known she was working for the red-nosed reindeer's boss.

Sophia waved to Ethan again, then backed away from the window, out of view. "Someone kill me."

Chelsea followed her into the living room. "I'll kill you after we open presents."

"Now?"

"Yes! Now! Then we can make breakfast. Pancakes, eggs, juice, coffee . . . And I might share some of it with you."

"Are you forgetting the stuff from the fridge is still over at Ethan's house?"

"Well then . . . *You* can go get it after we open the

presents."

They both knelt down in front of the tree, taking a few seconds to admire it. They wouldn't have even had that tree if it wasn't for Ethan. For an artificial tree, it was beautiful. Heck, Sophia was a sucker for any tree during Christmas—even Charlie Brown's tree.

Chelsea reached under the tree and grabbed the small green box with snowmen on it. She handed the box to Sophia. "Merry Christmas."

"Thanks." Sophia showed the paper no mercy, ripping it off in one fell swoop with a flick of the wrist.

Chelsea laughed. "You're brutal."

"Maybe I'm a little hungry." She set the paper aside and smiled at the gift. "Coco Chanel. How did you *ever* know I love this stuff?"

Chelsea shrugged. "I had a feeling . . . I tried to find you a hitman, but you won't *believe* how popular they are this year! People were fighting over them at the store like they were XBoxes."

Sophia laughed and reached over, hugging Chelsea. "Thank you."

"You're welcome."

The truth was Sophia needed little. Didn't need anything, really. Just having Chelsea close by was the best present she could ask for.

She handed Chelsea her gift and her sister unwrapped the small box carefully like she was afraid to break it.

"The box isn't that fragile," Sophia said. "Unless you're doing that to save the paper."

Chelsea didn't answer.

"Seriously? You're going to take the wrapping paper home with you?"

"Maybe . . ." She finally unwrapped it, set the paper aside and opened the small box.

"Jewelry?" Chelsea asked.

"I guess you'll find out."

Chelsea opened the box, peeking inside. Then she looked back up at Sophia. "Oh . . ." She pulled out the sterling silver necklace, then read what was etched on the attached leaf-shaped pendant. "A sister is a forever friend." Chelsea eyes moistened. "This is precious." She unclasped it and wrapped it around her neck. "I love it. Thank you." She hugged Sophia. "I love you. I wouldn't have been able to get through the divorce without you, you know that."

Sophia squeezed her tight. "We've got to stick together."

"Agreed! Oh, wait . . . one more thing" She reached under the tree and grabbed another package. "Here."

Sophia stared at the package. "We agreed that we would just exchange one gift. This is illegal and you're going to jail."

"You know I always have to get you at least one piece of clothing." Chelsea smiled her devious smile, which always scared Sophia because she knew it would be something she did not want to wear.

Sophia handed the package back. "We also agreed last

year you would not buy me any more Christmas clothing. Hope you saved the receipt."

"Okay, this is the last year. Promise."

"That's what you said last year."

Chelsea frowned. "So . . . You don't want it? Seasonal merchandise at that store is non-refundable."

"I'll pay you to destroy it."

Chelsea just stared at Sophia until the guilt made her cave.

"Fine." Sophia snatched the package back from Chelsea. "I'm telling you, you have a skill for the dramatic. You really need to get into movies."

"*Thank* you."

Sophia opened the package and pulled out the red sweatshirt and read the printing on the chest. "Santa's Favorite Ho." She stared at it and then busted out in laughter. "You seriously think I'll wear this?"

Chelsea laughed along with her. "Why not?"

"Why not? *Why* not? Just like that I went from Santa's helper to Santa's Ho."

Chelsea smirked. "Sounds like a promotion! Come on, this is fun. Try it on."

Sophia huffed and shook her head in disbelief. "The things I do for you."

"That's because you love me as much as I love you."

Sophia slipped the sweatshirt over her head and pulled the bottom down past her waist. "This has nothing to do with love. I'm only putting it on because it's freezing in here."

Chelsea pretended to inspect the sweatshirt. "It's you. It's *definitely* you. Promise you'll wear it all morning."

"Only if you make the pancakes."

"Only if you go across the way and get our things from Ethan's fridge."

"Deal." Sophia smiled at her sister. "You're a shrewd negotiator."

"You're not so bad yourself." Chelsea laughed and pointed to the sweatshirt. "You may want to cover that up though before you head across the way."

"*That* you can count on."

Sophia changed into her jeans, put on her boots, and threw on a thick down jacket over her gaudy new sweatshirt.

Three minutes later she rang Ethan's doorbell and waited.

"Woof!"

Sophia realized she hadn't even looked at herself in the mirror before she left the house. What did her hair look like?

"Woof!"

She quickly tried to straighten out her hair.

Too bad the front door opened before she could make it halfway manageable.

"Merry Christmas," Sophia said, dropping her hands to her side.

"Merry Christmas," Ethan replied, with a heart-thumping smile plastered across his face. He stepped toward

Sophia, then stopped abruptly. "Oh . . . Can I give you a Christmas hug or are you going to punch me in the face again?"

"I can't make any guarantees, but I will try my best to control my violent tendencies."

Ethan chuckled. "I appreciate that." He reached down to hug Sophia just as Bear stepped onto the porch and slammed into her.

"Oh, my God!" Sophia said, stepping back and covering her mouth with her hand.

She didn't punch him in the chin like the last time. No, this time was worse.

This time she head-butted his chin.

Ethan felt his jaw, most likely looking for blood or something broken. "Is this your way of telling me you're not an affectionate person?"

"That was an accident. Really."

He chuckled. "I'm not giving up on you. Okay, keep your hands to your side."

Sophia straightened out her arms.

"Don't move," he added. "I'm coming in."

"Not moving."

"Good." Ethan stepped closer once again and wrapped his arms around her in a hug she wished could have lasted a few hours. "Merry Christmas."

"Merry Christmas."

When was the last time I had a hug like that?

Sophia felt her temperature go up, even though she was standing on the porch in the cold. She would die if she was blushing while she was having a bad hair day. Surely Ethan would notice and that wasn't acceptable.

Time for a distraction.

She petted Bear on his head as his tongue attacked her other hand. "Hey, boy. How are you?"

"Bear, can you please stick your tongue back in your mouth and leave her alone for a moment?" Ethan gestured to the inside of his house. "Please. Come in."

"Thank you," Sophia said, stepping inside and wiping her hand on the side of her jeans. "Sorry for coming over so early. Chelsea wanted to make breakfast, so I needed to get the bag from your refrigerator downstairs."

"Not a problem. Let me run and get it and I'll be right back."

"Thank you."

Ethan disappeared downstairs.

"Woof!"

Bear followed right behind him.

Less than a minute later Ethan returned with the bag from the refrigerator. "Here you go."

"Thank you for doing that. I guess we'll see you in a few hours to go to the show."

"Yes."

"Okay then. Thanks again."

Back at the house, Chelsea had already pulled out the

pancake griddle and pancake mix. Sophia emptied the bag in the fridge and headed back outside to grab firewood.

She couldn't help but sneak a look up at Ethan's large family room window again as she headed along the path that paralleled the steep ravine between both houses. Sure, she had just seen him, but she didn't think she could ever get tired of looking at that man.

Ethan appeared in the window, startling Sophia. She wasn't sure if he could see her, but she pretended not to be looking and spun back around. That's when it all went wrong.

Sophia lost her balance and fell backwards off the path and down the ravine.

It was a long fall, most of it soft and fluffy.

Until she got to the bottom, that is. That's when her butt hit something hard. It would leave a bruise, whatever it was, but her ego would have the biggest bruise if Ethan had witnessed what had happened.

She tried to move and everything felt fine—she didn't think she had any broken bones, but something suddenly felt wet and freezing across her entire body. There was also the sound of trickling water. She was getting colder by the second.

Sophia stood and looked down at her jeans and down jacket. They were completely soaked through, along with her shoes and socks. She was already shivering. She tried climbing up the side of the ravine and slipped back down.

She tried a few more times to no avail. It was steeper than she thought.

"Sophia!" Ethan yelled. "Are you okay?"

"I'm okay," she lied, as her teeth chattered. She glanced up to the top of the ravine and could see how far she fell. "I'm just going to climb out of here and go back inside."

"I'm coming down."

"No!" she screamed, waving him off. "I can handle this."

Ethan didn't say another word and stood there waiting. She guessed he was just going to watch her try.

She took a few steps up side of the ravine and slid back down. She tried again, sliding to the bottom again.

Ethan blew out a breath. "I can help you."

"No."

"Why not?"

She placed her hands on her soaking wet and very cold hips. "Because you are *always* helping me."

"Why is that bad?"

"Because it is!"

"You're so stubborn."

"Tell me something I don't know."

"Soon you'll be a stubborn woman with hypothermia and frostbite."

She stared at him. Was he serious?

"Hang on," he said, disappearing. A few seconds later a rope landed at the bottom next to Sophia. "Grab the end of the rope and hold on tight."

"I don't need your help."

"Just do it."

"No."

"Grab the rope or I'm coming down there and I'll throw you over my shoulders."

"You wouldn't."

He stared at her.

I guess you would.

She grabbed the rope and held on tight.

Fine.

Ethan would save her again for the umpteenth time and there was nothing she could do about it.

With each tug of the rope she slid along the ravine walls, closer to the top. Just like that, she made it and Ethan lifted her to her feet.

Sophia opened and closed her frozen hands. "This doesn't make sense. How could I be so wet from the snow?"

"The bottom of that ravine is the runoff—snow melt from the mountain." He pointed to her clothes. "You need to get out of those clothes fast."

"I . . ." She trembled and hugged herself. "I'll be fine."

"That's it." He bent down, hooked one arm behind her knees, the other behind her back and lifted her into his arms. "We're changing your name to Lady Stubborn."

"Put me down."

"Not gonna happen."

She wrapped one arm around his shoulders and hooked

her hands together for stability. "*You're* the one who's stubborn."

He didn't respond and carried her across the path, up the stairs and into the house.

"Put me down now!"

"Fine!" He set her down and grabbed hold of the zipper under her chin, yanking it to her waist. Then he flipped her around and pulled the jacket off her in one swift motion.

"Hey!" she said, swinging back around. "Are you crazy?"

He glanced down at her *Santa's Favorite Ho* sweatshirt she forgot she was wearing underneath the jacket.

Before she had time to get embarrassed he grabbed her hands, cupped them together with his hands in front of his lips, and blew warm air into them. "You need to get into a warm bath now." He took another deep breath and blew another dose of warm air.

I could get used to this. Someone taking care of me. Pampering me.

Chelsea ran into the living room. "Why are you soaking wet? Oh my God, are you okay?"

Ethan dropped her hands. "She'd be okay if she just listened. She needs to get out of these clothes *now* or she can get hypothermia. Can you run a warm bath for her? Not too hot."

"Right away," Chelsea said, heading down the hallway to the bathroom.

Ethan pointed to Sophia. "You. Lady Stubborn. Get out of your clothes and get in the bath for thirty minutes. Now."

She opened her mouth to speak and he held up a finger to cut her off. "Not even a word, I swear. I will rip those clothes off you and drop you in the tub myself if I have to."

She stared at him for a moment.

Did he really just say that?

He stood there tapping his foot on the floor, a dead-serious look on his face.

It appeared he did say that.

She turned and walked to the bathroom.

Better if she did what she was told.

Better if she didn't tell him he was a pushy, pushy man.

I will rip those clothes off you and drop you in the tub myself if I have to.

Better if she didn't tell him that was the best offer she'd received in a long, long time.

Chapter Thirteen

A few hours later, Chelsea and Sophia were passengers in Ethan's truck on the way to the theater to see Violet's matinee performance of *A Charlie Brown Christmas*.

Ethan was quiet. Sophia thanked him for rescuing her again and he nodded.

Was he mad at her?

Ethan glanced over at her and then got his eyes back on the road. "How are you feeling, Sophia?"

"Good. Very good, actually. I didn't want to get out of the bath, but I was resembling a prune. Honestly, I didn't think I could get in trouble just outside the front door."

He nodded. "If you're prepared, you usually can stay out of trouble. Don't mess with Mother Nature. Promise me that."

"I promise."

He nodded again and his shoulders seemed to relax a little. "Good."

He was lecturing her, but he was right. She needed her hard head to soften before she got in trouble. She left it at that and decided to check her phone in case she had missed a text message or voicemail from Brad.

Sophia pulled her cell phone from her purse.

Chelsea leaned forward and reached from the back seat, slapping Sophia on the top of the hand.

"Ouch!" Sophia said, opening and closing her hand. "What did you do that for?"

"What happened?" Ethan asked, looking over at Sophia briefly before getting his attention back on the road. "Do you want me to pull over?"

"No," Chelsea said. "It's nothing. I thought I saw a bug on Sophia's hand."

"Highly unlikely in the winter here."

"I'm sure it was nothing. Sophia was just making sure her phone was turned off, so it doesn't make noise in the theater. Weren't you?"

"That's *exactly* what I was doing." Sophia twisted her body around so she was facing Chelsea in the back seat, then mouthed *you're dead* to her sister.

"Good idea," Ethan said. "My phone is already off."

"You don't have to work today?" Sophia asked, stuffing her phone back in her purse and changing the subject.

"I got someone to cover for me. Believe it or not, I've already seen Violet do this show ten times if you include dress rehearsals. I still can't believe what a natural she is. You'll see for yourself how the audience loves her and she seems to feed off it. She's a ham."

Sophia knew what that was like. She loved the theater, loved being onstage. It was so thrilling and magical and nerve-wracking all at the same time. There was nothing like that immediate response the actors got from the audience. It was like a shot of pure adrenaline straight to the veins. She was excited for Violet—for all the actors, actually—and looked forward to meeting them after the production.

Sophia stared out the window at the winter wonderland. "Is more snow expected?"

Ethan shook his head. "Not until around the new year, unfortunately."

Chelsea leaned forward from the back seat. "There's still not enough snow for the season?"

"Not even close. And when the temperature gets too high the snow turns to slush. That makes it more difficult for skiers and snowboarders to control their movements, which leads to more injuries. Avalanches can even occur under the same conditions."

"Wow, that sounds scary."

"It can be. That's why we like the cooler temperatures in the winter."

"How cool?"

"Twenty-five degrees is good. That's cold enough that the snow won't melt, but not *so* cold you freeze your buns off going up the gondola."

Sophia and Chelsea laughed and continued to admire the view out the window.

Lake Tahoe was a different lifestyle than Sophia was accustomed to, that was for sure. The one thing she noticed as Ethan drove them to the theater was that most people didn't seem to be in a hurry at all. Just about everyone drove the speed limit. Ethan was going five miles per hour *under* the limit. She wasn't going to say anything because she felt safe.

In Lake Tahoe, not only did she feel safer, she also felt healthier—which would probably sound weird if she ever mentioned that to anyone. Must be the fresh mountain air because she couldn't figure out why.

"Wow," Sophia said, admiring the theater as Ethan pulled into the parking lot. The marquee over the entrance displayed *A Charlie Brown Christmas* in large, bright letters. "No offense, but I was expecting something a lot smaller for a children's theater production."

"No offense taken," Ethan said, sticking the truck in park and pointing through the windshield toward the building. "Most people have the same reaction when they see it for the first time. This place is a big deal to us. We have parents who have moved here from out of the area or from out of state just so their children could attend the Young Conservatory. People have even compared it to the American Conservatory Theater in San Francisco."

"A.C.T. in San Francisco has an excellent reputation. Winona Ryder and Nicolas Cage studied there."

"Not a surprise . . . That just shows you how good these programs can be." He frowned. "Unfortunately, there have been some financial problems over the last year, plus the conservatory director, Melissa Stork, is retiring. The future of the theater company is up in the air. We're not giving up hope, though—hence the fundraiser."

She nodded. "Well, hopefully everything will work out."

"Yeah," Chelsea said. "I hope so, too."

He smiled. "Violet and the other kids love it, plus they're learning so much more than just acting. The classes are also designed to develop imagination, concentration, character, and professionalism. They take away so much from these programs—I'm sure you've noticed how mature Violet is for her age."

"Absolutely." Chelsea smiled. "She really blows me away."

Ethan chuckled. "Me, too. You'll be even *more* blown away once you've seen her onstage."

They got out of the truck and walked toward the theater. Sophia was becoming a big fan of the snow and fresh air. It was a far cry from the air she had to breathe in LA.

They entered the theater lobby and Sophia stopped to admire the oversized fireplace in the middle. A large group of people huddled around it, enjoying the warmth, and most likely talking about the show they were going to see or an actor they knew. A giant chandelier hung in the middle of the lobby and dark wood handrails made their way up the ramps on both sides leading to the balcony seating. It had a warm, inviting feeling, yet somehow could appear classy at the same time.

A woman over by the espresso cart pointed in Sophia's

direction and the two people with the woman turned and smiled. Sophia smiled back and followed Ethan.

They left their jackets with the coat check attendant and each of them received programs.

"Oh, great!" Sophia said, stopping and pointing to the woman standing behind the counter selling flowers. "We need to come back here after the show. I'd like to get flowers for Violet."

Chelsea lit up. "Me, too."

Ethan gave them both an approving smile. "That's sweet. Of course." He pointed to the double doors with the tuxedoed man taking tickets. "We can enter over there."

They entered the theater and were waved over by Mike and Uncle Al down in the third row.

Uncle Al stood and pointed to the seat next to him. "I would like to have the honor of sitting next to Sophia, if you don't mind."

"I don't mind at all," Sophia said, taking a seat in the chair next to Uncle Al. Ethan sat on the other side of her. Chelsea sat on the end next to Mike—which they both didn't seem to mind at all.

Sophia marveled at how Mike and her sister had hit it off so quickly. She wondered if there was a realistic possibility of the two of them ending up together. How could it be with both of them living so far away from each other? But she had to admit the more she saw Ethan, the more she wanted to see him. Almost as if she didn't care about the distance between them.

"*A Charlie Brown Christmas* premiered on CBS back on December ninth of 1965!" Uncle Al said.

"Here we go with the statistics," Mike said, chuckling. "Please tell us how many viewers watched that night. I'm sure you know."

"Of course I know," Uncle Al said, without missing a beat. "Over fifteen million! That was *a lot* of people back then for television viewing. Since then it has been the second longest-running television Christmas special of all time, behind *Rudolph the Red-Nosed Reindeer.*"

Ethan nudged Sophia on the side of the arm. "Your favorite!"

She nudged him right back. "*Your* favorite."

They enjoyed a laugh and a few minutes later the performance began.

Sophia eagerly awaited for Violet to appear. She knew what most of the kids were feeling backstage, waiting. She'd done it before plenty of times.

The thrill. The excitement. The nerves.

When Violet entered Sophia couldn't help but smile. She loved how she entered the scene with such confidence.

Funny how Sophia and Chelsea must have been thinking the same thing. They both looked over at Mike, wanting to get a glimpse of his expression as his daughter acted on stage. It was like watching the groom's face as the bride walks down the aisle toward him on their wedding day. Not a surprise that Mike's smile was wide, filled with love and pride.

Playing the part of Lucy, Violet wore a blue dress with puffed sleeves. Her black and white saddle shoes were cute and made her costume complete.

And Ethan was right, Violet was a natural.

It was amazing how much confidence and presence she had onstage at such a young age. There was something special about Violet, for sure, and Sophia wouldn't be surprised if she ended up being a big star. Hopefully the theater and its programs would stay open and give her the opportunity to grow even more as an actress.

During the second act Sophia and Ethan both moved their elbows up to the armrest between them, colliding.

Ethan didn't say a word. He pulled his arm back and gestured for her to use the armrest.

Sophia shook her head and gestured back for him to use it.

He shook his head no and pointed to the armrest.

She shook *her* head no and pointed to the armrest.

Then Ethan shrugged and turned his attention back to the stage.

Fine. I guess nobody will use it then.

A few seconds later Ethan reached over and grabbed Sophia's forearm, placing it on the arm rest and patting it.

It took all of her strength to keep from bursting out in laughter. This guy was something.

After the performance and the standing ovation, they headed to the lobby to buy the flowers and wait for Violet. One actor after another came from backstage to greet their smiling family and friends and take pictures.

Violet finally appeared and was swallowed up by her dad's embrace. "You knocked it out of the ballpark again, sweetie." Mike kissed the top of her head. "I'm proud of you."

"Thanks, Dad."

Both Ethan and Uncle Al gave her hugs and congratulations next.

Then Chelsea held out the flowers for Violet. "You were amazing."

"Thank you," Violet said, handing the flowers to her dad and hugging Chelsea. "And thank you for coming." Then she turned to Sophia. "Thank you for coming, Sophia."

"It was a pleasure." Sophia handed the flowers for Violet to Mike and hugged her. "And like Chelsea, I was impressed." She leaned in. "You were my favorite. Amazing, really."

Violet smiled. "Thank you." She turned to Mike and beamed. "I was her favorite."

"Not a surprise," Mike said, winking. He pointed to a few of the other actors who were walking in their direction. "We can keep that to ourselves, though."

"I know, Dad. Even kids have egos."

Three other actors gathered behind Violet, their eyes popping back and forth between Sophia and Violet. They didn't say a word, but Sophia knew the behavior. They wanted to meet her and were hoping Violet would introduce them. Kids were so cute at that age.

Violet pointed to the girl in front. "This is my best friend, Madison Lee. She played Sally, Charlie Brown's younger sister."

"I remember," Sophia said, smiling. "Great job."

"Thanks," Madison said. "I can't believe Lady Karma is here."

"Violet invited me," Sophia said.

"You know Violet?" the boy who played Charlie Brown asked.

Sophia smiled. "We spent Christmas Eve together."

All the kids looked at Violet in awe as she smiled proudly.

"Hey, you know what?" Sophia said, pulling her phone from her purse. "I would love a picture with all of these stars. Can someone take it?"

Smiles appeared on their faces and one kid even jumped up and down, excited to take a picture with Sophia.

Ethan held out his hand. "I can take it."

"Great." Sophia gathered the young actors closer so they'd all fit in the shot. "Take two or three of them and I'll share them with Violet so *she* can share them with everyone."

"Okay," Ethan said, positioning himself. "Everyone

say . . . Lady Karma."

"Lady Karma!" they all chorused as Ethan snapped a few shots.

The children gave their thanks and said their goodbyes, then Chelsea and Sophia followed Uncle Al, Mike, and Violet out to the parking lot.

"Oh," Ethan said, handing the phone back to Sophia. "I have your phone, Lady Karma. I assume that's how you would like me to address you from now on?"

She snagged the phone from his hand. "Only if you want to lose a few fingers."

Ethan chuckled. "I had *no* idea Santa's little helper could be so cruel."

Sophia stopped and stared at Ethan for a beat, not sure how to respond. This had to be one of the most embarrassing things ever. He'd seen her in her *Santa's Little Helper* pajamas.

She turned and pointed to Chelsea. "This is all *your* fault. You made me wear them. That's what cruel sisters do."

"Hey!" Chelsea said, placing her hands on her hips. "I put *a lot* of thought into that gift. Almost as much as I put in the one you got this morning."

Ethan arched an eyebrow. "Oh, you mean Santa's favorite—"

"That's it," Sophia said, grabbing Ethan's hand. "Say goodbye to your fingers."

Chapter Fourteen

The gondola ascended farther and farther up the mountain toward the observation deck at almost ten thousand feet above sea level. Sophia found it hard to focus on the sapphire-blue waters of Lake Tahoe below, or the surrounding snow-capped trees and mountains. She could blame that one hundred percent on the man who was standing behind her—up *against her* was more like it.

How did she end up on the gondola with Ethan? And why was she enjoying his company more and more with each day that passed?

Somebody slap me, I must be losing it.

How it came to be that they were together on the gondola was kind of a blur—it all happened so quickly, really. She tried to think back to what had happened.

One minute they were in the parking lot of the theater talking about how wonderful Violet was in *A Charlie Brown Christmas*, then Chelsea mentioned she was looking forward to going snowshoeing with Mike and Violet.

Then in *another* way-too-obvious sisterly set-up, or maybe betrayal was a better word, Chelsea suggested that Sophia take the gondola up to the top of the mountain with Ethan.

How could Sophia say no when Ethan smiled and responded with, "I'd love to."

Really, it was the accompanying smile that left her defenseless.

Ethan's smile was a weapon.

The man needed to be arrested for carrying it without a license, or at least be fined for carelessly throwing it around without regard for the consequences or destruction it would cause to any female in its path.

She sensed her heart was in danger and heading for a complete meltdown.

"Almost there," he whispered from behind, causing her heart to skip a beat. "How do you like it so far?"

How do I like what so far? The warmth of your breath in my ear? Your clean, fresh scent that is part musky and part sweet? How do I like the way who-knows-what-part-of-your-body keeps bumping into my butt with every slight movement of the gondola? Let me be honest. I love it. Love it, love it, love it!

"Sophia?"

"Oh . . ." She tried to concentrate and give him a simple answer knowing full well he was just asking about the view and the experience of riding the gondola and nothing more. "It's captivating. I love it."

Love it, love it, love it!

A few minutes later the gondola arrived at the observation deck, a fourteen thousand square foot mid-station platform with a cafe and gift shop.

They stepped out of the gondola and were immediately engulfed with the biting cold mountain air. Sophia pulled her beanie lower over her ears as they headed to the overlook.

The panoramic view was breathtaking, offering shore-to-shore views of Lake Tahoe and Carson Valley. The vastness and striking blue tones of the lake were mesmerizing.

She took a deep breath of cold air and let it out. "I don't think I've ever seen anything so beautiful before in my entire life."

"Me, neither."

If Sophia were to ever fantasize about Ethan, he would have been looking *at her* when he said that, but there was no way she was going to turn to see where his eyes were focused.

"That's why I live here," he added, destroying any chance of a potential fantasy.

Still, they took more than a few pictures and admired the magic of Lake Tahoe from way up above. It was getting late in the afternoon, so Sophia suggested going to get warmed up with a cup of coffee inside Cafe Blue. Ethan thought it was a great idea.

A few minutes later they were both seated at a table for two inside the cafe, Sophia with her latte and Ethan with his mocha.

He took a sip of his mocha and sighed. "Hmm—that hits the spot." He shot her a smile. "You enjoying yourself?"

She smiled, nodded, and took a sip. "Very much."

He took another sip. "Good. So . . . tell me about *you* if

you don't mind."

"What would you like to know?"

Ethan thought about it for a beat. "Where did you grow up?"

Sophia was surprised by that question. Most people knew everything about her from the newspapers, entertainment shows on television, from her profile on Wikipedia, or just from searching her name on Google. It was amazing to her that he knew *nothing* about her.

Ethan felt like a real person to her. Unpretentious. Authentic. It was wonderful and such a refreshing change from the men in Los Angeles.

"I'm a native Southern California girl," Sophia answered. "You?"

"I'm a native *Northern* California boy. What about school?"

"Beverly Hills High School, then UCLA where I got my bachelor of arts degree in theater. Your turn."

"South Tahoe High School," he said. "No college."

She nodded. "So what did you do after you graduated from high school then? Straight into the workforce?"

He shook his head. "I trained at the North American Ski Training Center for the US Olympic Team."

She sat up in her chair. "Wow. I'm impressed."

"Don't be. I failed miserably." He took another sip of his mocha but didn't continue.

She set her latte down and leaned forward. "You're not

going to leave me hanging like that, are you?"

Ethan cocked his head to the side. "What do you mean?"

"*I mean* you said you were training for the Olympic team, that you failed miserably, but you have to tell me what happened!"

"You don't want to know."

"Yes. I *do* want to know."

"No, you don't."

"How long are we going to play this?"

"How long will it take until you give up?"

"That's just it, I *won't* give up."

He studied her and nodded. "Okay, but only because you're a stubborn woman and I fear that you'll punch me in the face again."

She smiled. "I can accept that. What happened?"

He took another sip of his mocha, looking like he was contemplating where he wanted to start the story. Why was he being so melodramatic? Whatever happened couldn't be that bad, could it?

"I had made amazing progress with the training, and my coaches said I was doing very well," Ethan said, his energy dropping. "And then . . ."

"And then . . .?"

"Then one day I was backcountry skiing over on Donner Summit to get away from the weekend crowds, but that was something I had agreed not to do while in training.

And I injured myself."

"How did you injure yourself?"

"I was skiing in a zone called *The Bubbles*, which is strictly for expert skiers under stable avalanche conditions. Halfway down I heard a scream and found a teenage girl who crashed and hurt her leg. She was right on the edge of a drop and was slipping toward it."

"Oh, my God. What did you do?"

"I tried to rescue her."

This is sounding familiar. "Go on."

"I stepped out of my bindings and made my way over— it wasn't easy because gravity works against you when you're descending, plus the snow was harder because it was a north-facing slope. If you lean back your feet may slip out from under you. Keeping a slightly bent knee improves balance and reduces the risk of knee injury." He stared at her for a beat. "Sorry, I'm getting technical and don't want to bore you. You want something to eat?"

"I'm not interested in food at the moment and you're not boring me. Please continue. I want to know what happened."

"Well, she shouldn't have been anywhere near that area. It was *way* above her skill level and steep as hell. I tried to rescue her but kept slipping. Then I planted my foot wrong, lost my balance, and tore my meniscus. My biggest mistake was not considering the snow conditions before I tried to help her." His eyes became dull and wet. "And because of that she paid the price . . . with her life."

Ethan looked away and stared blankly out the window.

Sophia threw her hands over her mouth. "No."

He turned back to Sophia and nodded. "You shouldn't mess with Mother Nature."

Oh, my God.

That's why he was so upset with her when she fell down the ravine, even more upset when she didn't listen to him when he told her to get out of those cold, wet clothes.

She couldn't imagine the mental anguish Ethan must have gone through, was *still* going through. He tried to rescue a girl and ended up losing her, plus crushed his own dreams of being on the US Olympic Ski team because of the injury he sustained while trying to save her. It didn't seem fair. But what also wasn't fair was him blaming himself for her death. He was just skiing and stumbled upon her by coincidence. He had tried his best and couldn't do it.

Sophia reached across the table and grabbed Ethan's hands, holding them tightly. "How can you blame yourself for that? It wasn't your fault."

He pulled his hands free from hers. "I could have been more prepared."

"Hey, I know CPR and the Heimlich maneuver in case someone chokes, but I don't think I'm capable of saving a person from any other random accident or health problem."

"I am."

She cocked her head to the side. "How?"

"After I recovered from my surgery, I made the vow and commitment to never let that happen again. I signed up for every indoor and outdoor safety program I could find: first aid, emergency response, beginner, intermediate and advanced fundamentals of search and rescue, advanced avalanche safety course, outdoor survival, you name it. Now I'm able to help search for lost or injured skiers, respond to plane crashes, stranded climbers, river rescues, fires, just about anything. That's why I volunteered with the South Tahoe Action Team."

"That's amazing. How long did all of that training take?"

"Almost six years. I'm also a certified EMT, trained to recognize signs and symptoms of illness or injury and give the appropriate emergency treatment."

Sophia didn't know what to say. The man was amazing. Talk about a tragedy changing the course of someone's life. But he still seemed to carry some of the guilt of what happened with that girl, even though it wasn't his fault.

"That was a tragedy," she said. "But because of it, you can do good and save lives."

"I would give up everything I have and everything I am in a heartbeat to have that girl back and alive today."

Sophia stared at Ethan, deep in thought. She'd honestly never met a man like him before, so kind, compassionate, and selfless. And then there were his ridiculous physical attributes that made her want to reach across the table and kiss him right there in that cafe. It was just as she suspected earlier. No. Even worse now. Her heart was in danger of being stolen and the thief was sitting across from her with a mocha in his hands.

What the hell just happened there?

Ethan looked away from Sophia's indescribable gaze and wondered why the hell he had opened his heart to her that way. He had kept that story locked up inside of him for years and thought he had thrown away the key. That wasn't even something he had mentioned to Lorraine when they were together. But that sexy actress from Hollywood just reached into his heart and pulled it out of him. Just like that.

And why didn't he have the mental hangover this time, like he normally did whenever he thought of that day he couldn't save the girl? He had a moment of sadness, but then his thoughts were back on Sophia, fascinated by her, wanting to know more about her.

Sophia reached across the table for the second time and placed her hands over the top of his. "You're a special man, Ethan Woods."

Those words comforted him. Ever since he could remember he'd always wanted to do the right thing, to treat people with respect, to help someone in need. Not that he wanted anything in return or needed validation, but it felt good to hear someone appreciate you as a person and for what you were doing.

"Thank you," he answered. "Does this mean I am back to Superman status?"

She smiled. "Yes. You are officially a superhero."

He pumped his fist in the air. "Yes! Finally."

She laughed and took another sip of her latte. "I'm curious about something . . ."

"What?"

"What do you do for work when it's not ski season and you can't give lessons?"

"Mike and I run a business together May through October. Water sports and boat tours on Lake Tahoe. Waterskiing, wakeboarding, tubing, rentals, lessons, pretty much anything on the water."

"That sounds like a lot of fun."

"It is. My life is all about the outdoors and I wouldn't have it any other way."

She nodded. "You have a *very* fascinating life."

"I can't complain at all, really. But then again, *your* life seems to be fascinating, too. In fact, I'm curious how you went from attending UCLA to becoming *Lady Karma*."

"After graduation I did a year of theater in Los Angeles before landing a role in a Broadway show. Two years on Broadway, then I auditioned and landed the leading role for *Lady Karma*. The rest is history."

"Did you have any idea you would become a star when

you were attending UCLA?"

She laughed. "No. I mean, we all have dreams of becoming working actors and making enough to pay the bills, but the reality is about ninety percent of all actors are unemployed at any given time. With that percentage you need to have confidence, drive, and talent if you want to have any chance of making it. UCLA is known around the world for their school of theater, film, and television. I decided in my sophomore year in high school that their training would hopefully give me an edge over others in the field and that the time and investment would be worth it."

"You called that one correctly, although there's no such thing as a sure thing. Are there any other success stories from UCLA?"

"Ben Stiller, Tim Robbins, Carol Burnett, and James Dean, to name a few."

"So, nobody then."

She laughed. "Maybe you would be more impressed with Jaleel White?"

He had no idea who Jaleel White was.

She obviously noticed the confused expression on his face and clarified. "You know, Urkel? From the sitcom *Family Matters.*"

"Urkel!" He nodded his approval. "Urkel was a genius."

Sophia laughed again and took the last sip of her latte. "That he was." She shook the empty cup and then set it on the table. "All done."

"Would you like another one?"

Hopefully she would say yes. Ethan wasn't ready for his time with Sophia to be over.

"I'd rather not," she said. "I don't want to spoil my appetite for dinner."

"Sorry, I didn't realize you had dinner plans. I guess we should head back down then."

"Oh, I don't have plans. I just like to have a good appetite when I'm ready to eat, that's all."

Ethan didn't think he would get a better opening than that to spend more time with Sophia. He didn't want it to end there, so he needed to take a chance and ask.

"Okay, then." Ethan scratched the side of his face. "You up for something else?"

She smiled. "Like what?"

"There's a cool little dive bar where the locals go for the best hot dogs and beer in a one-mile radius."

She laughed. "Sounds impressive."

"That's nothing. They even have a pool table."

"Now you've got my attention."

"So you like hot dogs?"

"Love them."

Ethan clasped his hands together. "I just want to spend more time with you, so we can go anywhere you want. I like you." He almost fell over from the sudden kick in his heart rate. He'd pretty much laid it on the line and told her how he felt, because he did feel something.

Something strong.

Maybe it was a pipe dream that someone like her would go out with someone like him, but he would never know if he didn't ask. Her hesitation to give him an answer wasn't a good sign. What was going on in that pretty head of hers? Now he was sure his heart was pumping blood at maximum speed.

She bit her lower lip. "You like me, huh?"

He nodded. "A lot."

"Even with all of the *supposed* stubbornness you claim I'm full of?"

He grinned. "Even with it. Crazy, right?"

She laughed. "Crazy, indeed. But what's probably even crazier is . . . I like you, too."

"God, you're right. That *is* crazy." He tilted his head to the side. "So then, the question is . . . what are we going to do with this madness of you liking me and me liking you?"

She shrugged. "The only thing we *can* do. We need to go to that dive bar."

Chapter Fifteen

Sophia tried to contain her excitement as Ethan parked his truck on the street in front of Dylan's Dive Bar. She surprised herself by agreeing to go with him. The best part was she didn't feel guilty about not being with Chelsea because she knew her sister would approve.

In fact, all of this was happening because of Chelsea.

Ethan pulled the front door open to Dylan's and waved Sophia through. "After you."

"Thank you," Sophia said, stepping in front of him to go inside before coming to a stop and looking around. The place was lively, a surprise for Christmas night. People were playing darts, shuffleboard, and pool. There was an older couple dancing in the middle of the floor to Dean Martin's version of "Baby, It's Cold Outside" playing on the sound system.

They took off their jackets and scarves and hung them on the rack at the end of the bar before sliding onto the stools in front of the bartender.

The female bartender made her way over to their side of the bar and smiled. "Merry Christmas."

"Merry Christmas," Ethan and Sophia said together.

Ethan leaned up closer to the bar. "We would like two of your *finest* hot dogs and two beers." He swiveled to Sophia. "Do you have a preference for beer?"

"Cold."

"My kind of woman."

"I like her, too," the bartender said. "But not as much as my daughter." She winked at Sophia and slid down to the other end of the bar to get their beers.

A minute later the bartender slid two mugs of cold beer down the bar, one stopping in front of Sophia and the other in front of Ethan.

"Give me about ten minutes for the hot dogs," said the bartender.

Ethan gave her a thumbs-up. "We'll be playing pool."

They grabbed their mugs and headed to the pool table in the corner. Luckily another couple had just finished a game and were leaving. Ethan placed his beer on the cocktail table against the wall and racked up the balls. Then he pulled two cue sticks off the wall, handing one of them to Sophia.

Sophia gave him a tsk tsk. "I pick my stick."

"Ahhh," he said, placing her cue stick back on the wall. "You're a pool shark, aren't you? I'm in serious trouble."

She inspected a few cue sticks before choosing one and chalking the tip. "I guess you'll find out."

Sophia knocked in three balls on the break, then knocked in two more.

Ethan chuckled. "Yeah, I'm definitely in trouble."

The bartender yelled across the room. "Two Dylan's dogs!"

"Perfect timing," Ethan said, gesturing toward the food. "A little food break should throw your game out of whack."

"Keep dreaming," Sophia said, shaking her head. "I'm going to kick your butt."

Ethan turned his back on her and stuck his butt out, placing his palms on the wall. "Well then, here you go. All yours."

The man was now flirting with her and she couldn't help but look down and check out his amazing butt. She also couldn't help slapping him hard in the same spot.

"Go get the food," she said, giggling.

"We haven't finished this conversation. I like the direction it's headed." Ethan grinned and picked up the tray from the bar with their hot dogs and condiments.

Sophia still couldn't believe she had slapped him on the butt. And she also couldn't believe how much she had enjoyed it.

Ethan returned a few seconds later and placed the tray on the table. "You're in for a treat. Dig in."

Sophia grabbed the bottle of mustard and squirted two even lines on each side of the dog. "Smells good."

Ethan pointed to her hot dog. "That's some precise mustard application if I've ever seen it."

Sophia laughed. "I don't mess around." She took a bite

and chewed slowly.

Ethan watched her, not touching his own hot dog yet. "Well?"

She nodded. "Amazing."

Ethan grabbed the bottle of ketchup, squirted two even lines on each side of the dog.

Sophia was about to take another bite but stopped. "Are you making fun of the way I apply condiments?"

"Not at all. Just wanted to see if your way would enhance the flavor of the dog."

"It *would* if you used mustard. Doesn't work with ketchup."

"That's the most ridiculous thing I've ever heard."

"You'll see. Go ahead. Take a bite."

He took a bite and chewed, his eyes not leaving Sophia. "Mmm. *So* good."

"Ha!" she said, taking another bite and moaning extra loud to prove a point.

Ethan chuckled. "You're a very cool woman when you're not so stubborn and constipated, as your sister likes to call you."

"And you're very cool when you're being Superman and *not* being so pushy."

He set his hot dog on the table and stepped closer, not saying a word. Sophia couldn't get a good read on him, but part of her wanted to believe he was going to kiss her.

Yes, please.

"I hope you don't mind me being forward," he said, raising his hand toward her cheek. "I've been wanting to do this for the last few minutes."

I've been wanting you to do it for the last few hours! Kiss me good!

Ethan moved a few strands of hair away from her mouth, tucking them behind one ear. "There. Got it." He broke eye contact with her, returning to his hot dog.

That's it? You can't be serious!

Frustrated, Sophia finished her hot dog and then finished off Ethan, making every single shot she took. She walked around the table and pulled the balls out of the pockets for the second game.

Ethan took a sip of his beer and then racked up the balls for the next game. "It would be nice if you gave me some playing time."

"You can always hope," she said, chalking up the tip of her cue stick.

Sophia stopped chalking when a woman approached, her eyes zeroed in on Ethan. She wore tight jeans and a top cut so low her girls looked like they wanted to come out and play.

"Hey there, Ethan," the woman said. "Long time no see."

Ethan slid the rack back under the table. "Hey, Trish."

"Last Christmas" by Wham! started playing on the sound system

"You wanna dance? Trish asked.

Sophia felt a pang of jealousy and stepped toward Ethan. "Honey, you promised me this dance."

Ethan shrugged at the woman and grabbed Sophia's hand. "Sorry, I forgot." He led her to the middle of the floor, spun her around, then wrapped his hand across her lower back. "You called me honey."

"Don't make a big deal of it . . .honey." Sophia smiled. "Any New Year's resolutions?"

Ethan raised an eyebrow, but Sophia was probably more surprised than he was that she had asked that question. She knew why she'd asked it; she wanted to know about his plans for the future and this was an roundabout way of getting the info without directly asking for it.

"I don't do New Year's resolutions," he answered.

Sophia stopped dancing and stared at him. "Really?" she said, not willing to leave it at that. "What's that all about?"

"Why would I want to change anything? I'm living the dream."

Sophia was skeptical that anyone's life could be perfect. Sure, you could have many things going well, but not wanting to improve or change a thing in your life? That was hard to believe.

She studied him for a moment. "And what do you consider *the dream*?"

"I've got an amazing life. Low key. Zero stress. I live in nature. I've got health, happiness, and peace. What more could I ask for?'"

He looked like a happy person overall, that was for sure. But what he said almost sounded rehearsed, like it was his go-to answer whenever someone inquired about his life.

Was he really that happy and relaxed?

What made little sense was why such a kind, good-looking man like Ethan didn't have a woman or a wife in his life. The curiosity was getting to her and she had to call him on it.

"So you're living the dream, huh?" Sophia asked.

"That's what I said. Yup. Can we start moving again? I thought you wanted to dance to this . . . Honey."

"I do."

"Good." He spun her around and smiled, then pulled her close again.

It felt wonderful to be in his arms, but there was something more important on her mind. "Why is it that a guy like you isn't married?"

"A guy like me? What kind of guy is a guy like me?"

She shrugged. "Attractive. Kind. I could probably come up with a few more adjectives, but you get my point."

He inched a little closer to Sophia and grinned. "I guess I could ask the same thing about you. Why isn't a girl like *you* married? And I'll save you the trouble of asking and say you are one of the most *beautiful* women I have laid eyes on. You're smart. You're successful. You're funny. Why aren't *you* married already?" He grinned and waited for an answer.

Sophia swallowed hard and contemplated calling the cops to arrest him for that smile that continued to weaken her defenses. That was interesting what he did there—how he turned the tables on her and she suddenly found it difficult to breathe.

"No answer?" he added.

She stood up taller. "I asked you first."

"Fair enough. My last girlfriend cheated on me—with an actor, actually. That pretty much ripped a hole in my heart a mile wide. So I decided I would just do my own thing, cruise, enjoy life, and avoid women. Until you came along, that is."

She stopped dancing again, staring at him for a moment. They were getting intimate here.

"You stopped dancing again," Ethan said.

She crinkled her nose. "Sorry. I need to stop doing that."

"No problem. So what about you? Why aren't you married with five hundred babies?"

She snorted. "I only want a hundred. Get your facts straight."

He nodded but didn't speak.

"I don't want some pity party from you when I tell you this, but it's not easy being me. When just about everyone knows who you are it's hard to tell if they're being real. It's hard to trust. It's hard to let them in, because I've been screwed over before. That was one of the fascinating things when I met you. You didn't know who I was. I loved that because *you* were real. You treated me like a normal person and called me on my bullshit when you thought I was stubborn which, since we are being honest, I will admit that *maybe* I am just a little."

"Or a lot."

She nodded and smiled. "Or a lot. Part of being here is a fantasy because I crave a simple life, I crave being a normal person. But that's just it, it's a fantasy."

"You *are* a normal person. When I see you I don't see some hot shot movie star. I see Sophia, a very likable person who deserves to be happy. If you don't like your lifestyle, why don't you make a change? Or if you have to, just give it up."

"You mean like give up everything and move to Lake Tahoe?"

"Or *anywhere*. Do *anything*. You're a smart woman. Follow your heart. What do you want?"

Not long ago she would have answered she wanted an Academy Award without hesitation. Now she wasn't so sure. Could she just give up everything in Hollywood? That seemed crazy. What was also crazy was she hadn't checked her phone in a while for text messages and voicemails from her agent. She hadn't been so obsessed with the Academy Award. And she was sure that was because there was a hunky man in Lake Tahoe that had been distracting her.

What did she want? Good question.

She glanced up at Ethan's lips as he stood there patiently waiting for her to say something. Anything. If she was being honest, right now the only thing she wanted was for Ethan to take her in his arms and kiss her until she passed out from the passion.

That's *exactly* what she wanted.

Ethan stepped closer, almost reading her mind.

She swallowed hard.

Was this happening? Were they going to kiss? Last time he teased her, so he'd better not do it again.

Kiss me.

Ethan closed the gap, now inches apart. "Sophia?"

"Yes," she said, barely audible.

"The Chipmunks are playing now. Do you really want to dance to the Chipmunks?"

There went that romantic moment. Gone in a flash. Maybe that was a sign.

They walked back to the corner to the pool table and Ethan grabbed a stick.

"Look," Sophia said. "Whatever it is we're doing here may not be such a good idea."

"Playing pool?"

"You and me. This is crazy."

"We already established it was crazy up at the top of the mountain, but that doesn't mean it's bad or that we shouldn't do it."

"I don't know. I mean—you live *here*." She pointed toward the front door. "And *I* live way over *there*." She pointed in the opposite direction and sighed.

Ethan followed the direction of her pointing finger. "You live in the corner of the bar?"

Sophia smacked him on the arm. "You know what I mean."

"I've never been one to force anything and I'm sure not going to start now, but doesn't something feel really right between us?"

She thought about it for a few seconds. "Yeah. It sure does."

"Okay, well just think about that tonight. I'll take you back now, but I would like to see you again tomorrow. I want to take you somewhere and I guarantee you'll love it."

"That's a bold statement."

He grinned. "I'm a bold guy."

Chapter Sixteen

Sophia glanced over at Ethan as he drove her to an undisclosed location the next morning. "You've never heard of sleeping in?"

Ethan chuckled. "I slept in."

"I think you need to look up the meaning of sleeping in because *your* definition is definitely different from *mine*."

When Ethan had taken Sophia home last night after Dylan's Dive Bar, he had walked her to her door and kissed her on the cheek. Then he said he would be back at eight in the morning to take her somewhere he knew she'd love. That meant she would have to get up at seven to get ready.

Getting up at seven in the morning while on vacation should be illegal.

Still, she couldn't say no to Ethan. She wanted to see him again, even if she had had some serious doubts last night. She still didn't know how they could have any possibility of a relationship, but a little voice inside her told her to stuff the doubts in a box, then burn the box.

Besides, she could just go out with Ethan and have fun, right? Maybe a little kissing too, while they were at it?

The only problem she saw with that theory was she had

feelings for the man now. She knew the feelings well and also knew it wouldn't be long before those feelings got stronger. Soon she would be head over heels for the man if she wasn't careful and didn't cut it off. But she didn't want to cut it off, that was the problem.

The torture.

Ethan drove past a large sign that said Heavenly Ice and pulled into the empty parking lot. He parked in the space directly in front of the entrance of the building. Then he killed the ignition, twisted toward her and grinned. "Okay, let's do this."

She glanced through the windshield at the front door with big letters that said the same words—Heavenly Ice.

"We're going to eat ice cream at eight in the morning? I *love* ice cream just as much as the next person, but I think *you* may have an eating disorder if you think this is normal."

He swung his door open and got out, chuckling. "You're a funny girl. Come on. We don't have that much time."

She got out of the truck and followed him. "Not much time before the cops arrive? This place isn't even open. Are you planning on breaking in?"

Ethan pulled a loose key from his pocket and dangled it in the air. "Not quite." He unlocked the front door and held it open for Sophia to pass through. Once inside he locked it and walked over to a wall unit. He opened it and flicked a few switches.

She glanced up at the sign on the wall behind the

counter.

Ice Skating Rules.

"Oh, my God," Sophia said. "This is an ice skating rink."

"*That* it is."

"We're going to ice skate?" she asked. "Now?"

"That was the plan." Ethan walked around to the other side of the counter and faced her, like an employee. "That's why we had to get up early. There's a local hockey team that comes in at nine thirty for practice, so we don't have a lot of time."

She glanced around the lobby. "Do you own this place?"

"No. I know the guy who owns it. I gave both of his daughters ski lessons when they were little and they're both skiing competitively now. He was grateful and said I could use the rink anytime I wanted. I called him and told him I met an amazing woman I wanted to sweep off her feet. Shoe size?"

"Seven."

He grinned. "How cute."

"So you plan on sweeping me off my feet, do you?"

"I do. Prepare to be swept." He opened a large door behind the counter and walked inside a room filled with rows and rows of ice skates. He grabbed two pairs of ice skates and handed her one, then waved her toward the double doors on the right. "Follow me." He stopped abruptly and set his skates on the floor. "Oh, wait a moment." He ran back behind the counter and pressed another button, then twisted a knob to the right.

Music began to play.

Ethan smiled and walked back toward her, picking up his skates. "Much better." He swung one of the double doors open and waved her through.

Sophia passed through the door and stopped inside, all the while admiring the huge ice skating rink in front of her. Giant lighted snowflakes the size of bowling balls were strung all around the rink. They sparkled to the beat of the music.

Sophia sat on the bench next to Ethan and laced up her skates. She glanced over at Ethan and smiled. He smiled back, but no words were spoken.

That's when she noticed her heartbeat had sped up.

She was nervous. Anxious. Excited.

Ethan stood and held out his hand.

She grabbed onto it and stood.

Still no words, but it felt natural. Comfortable.

He continued to hold her hand, leading her toward the rink. They stepped onto the ice and glided a few feet, then skated side-by-side. First slowly, getting used to the ice and the skates, then picking up the pace a little. Not too fast, not too slow.

Still holding hands.

She took a deep breath and let it out slowly, glancing up at the sparkly snowflakes hanging all around them. They were beautiful and this experience was amazing, even though it had only just started.

Ethan flipped around so he was skating backwards and grabbed her other hand.

She loved the feeling of him holding both of her hands. "You're good."

He shrugged. "I had training just in case there was ever a call for an ice rescue."

"Superman."

He chuckled and then tugged on her hands, letting them go as she flew past him on the ice.

She let out a little scream, not because she was scared but because it was so much fun.

He sped up and passed her, taking the turn and not looking back.

She took that as an invitation to race so she picked up the pace, skating to "Rockin' Around the Christmas Tree" by Brenda Lee.

It was wonderful, invigorating, and fun as she passed him around the next turn.

"Hey!" he called out from behind. "What do you think you're doing?"

Sophia laughed. "Making you look bad."

She continued to skate ahead of him, feeling more exhilaration with each stride.

They skated for another fifteen minutes, not talking much, just enjoying the experience.

Then Sophia felt Ethan's hands slip under the sides of her jacket, grabbing onto her waist from behind.

She couldn't see him, only feel his touch.

The cool temperature of the ice rink didn't feel so cool anymore as warmth and electricity from his hands spread quickly throughout her body. She'd suddenly lost the motivation to skate, almost paralyzed by his touch. Her legs stopped moving and they finally glided to a stop. All thoughts were on his hands and how wonderful they felt on her body, but she wanted to look into his eyes.

She grabbed his hands from her waist and set them free, then turned around to face him. There he was, the object of her desire. There was hunger in his eyes, even more than last night when she thought he would kiss her. She was certain it would happen now, and she craved that kiss more than anything in the whole world.

Ethan grabbed her waist again and pulled her body to his. He kissed her on the left cheek, then on the right, his eyes on her lips the entire time. He brushed his lips against hers, softly, slowly. It was his moan and the licking of his lips that almost did her in.

Complete torture.

Sophia wanted that kiss and she wanted it right then and there.

And she finally got it.

Ethan pressed his lips to hers gently, until she let him in. Then he deepened the kiss as she ran her hands up his chest, wrapping them around his neck. She moaned and didn't want it to end. The kiss was out of this world.

She couldn't remember ever experiencing something so wonderful, so romantic. She couldn't begin to describe the level of happiness she was feeling. Maybe ecstasy was a better word.

Two hours later Sophia was still buzzing from the kiss. She was disappointed when the employees and the hockey team showed up at the rink and they had to get off the ice. She could've stayed there all day with Ethan. She wanted to do it again.

Not exactly the ice skating, but the intimacy they shared.

"You're touching your lips again," Chelsea said from her reading chair. "I'm getting jealous because Mike and I haven't kissed yet."

Sophia had no idea she was touching her lips. She needed to stop doing that. The power of Ethan's kisses were affecting her long after they finished.

They were just as lethal as his smile.

"Sorry," Sophia said, placing her hands on her lap and trying to keep them there. "How come you haven't kissed yet?"

"Well, we almost did while we were shoe-skiing yesterday afternoon but, you know, Violet was there and . . ."

She shrugged. "We almost did last night at dinner too, but . . ."

"Violet?"

She nodded. "She's a smart girl so she knows something is going on between us, but we need to be sure about what's going on so she doesn't get hurt."

Sophia caught herself lifting her fingers to her lips again and dropped them back down to her lap. "Are you sure?"

"Me? Absolutely. Mike? He's on the fence. He said he really likes me, but the distance between our homes is a huge concern."

"And you don't have that concern?"

"Not even. I'd move here in a heartbeat."

Sophia wished she were just as certain as her sister, but she wasn't. As much as she loved Ethan's company and his kisses, she still wondered how this would all end.

Soon her vacation would be over.

Then what?

That was the million dollar question.

"Then I can find a job here," Chelsea said. "I can adapt to anything if I'm happy and have the motivation. It will happen soon, I know that."

Sophia squished her eyebrows together. "What will happen soon?"

"The kiss between me and Mike. He's cooking dinner for me tomorrow night and got a sitter for Violet. That's a guaranteed kiss when a man cooks for a woman, whether he wants it or not. And if for some strange reason it *doesn't* happen tomorrow, it has to on New Year's Eve. Everyone has to kiss on New Year's Eve—come on."

"Oh, that's right. New Year's! I can't believe I forgot about it. Did you make plans with him?"

She shook her head. "He asked me if I had plans and I told him not yet. But I told him whatever I do would involve *you* because I wanted to enter the new year with the person who stood by me during one of the shittiest years of my life."

Sophia stood and walked over to Chelsea. "Get up. I need to hug you."

Chelsea stood and Sophia wrapped her arms around her. She loved her sister so much. Even when they were younger, they were close and used to hug each other just like this. Like the hug would get them through the most difficult times. They had each other's backs, and the support was unconditional.

"Are you going to see Ethan later?" Chelsea asked, plopping back down in the chair and stretching the blanket over the length of her legs.

"Not today."

"He's giving afternoon ski lessons?"

"No. Volunteer day with the South Tahoe Action Team. It's only a four-hour shift, but he said he would text me in the afternoon around three."

"Texting? Wow. This sounds serious."

Sophia picked up a pillow and hurled it at Chelsea.

"Knock it off."

Chelsea set the pillow aside. "But seriously, that sounds so heroic, the *action* team."

Sophia chuckled and placed two more pieces of wood on the fire. "Yeah, I call him Superman."

"He's amazing, the things he does for others. That can be dangerous."

Sophia thought about Ethan's story of how he lost that woman trying to save her. That had to be the most horrible feeling in the world, watching someone die. Especially when there was nothing you could do about it. Chelsea didn't know the story and Sophia wasn't sure she wanted to tell her, but she did. They kept nothing from each other.

"Ethan lost a woman while he was trying to rescue her. She died."

Chelsea set her book down. "That's horrible."

"Yeah. I know. Imagine watching the person die."

Chelsea sighed. "I don't even want to imagine that. But it's amazing—people put their lives on the line everyday protecting and helping others. I admire and respect a person who is so selfless."

"Me, too."

The sound of a car door closing got Sophia's attention. She took a few steps toward the window and looked outside.

Ethan was backing out of his driveway and he seemed to be in a hurry. He backed his truck right into a snowbank, then spun his wheels and took off.

"That's weird."

Chelsea turned to Sophia. "What?"

"Ethan just left and he was in a hurry. He doesn't usually speed, so that was surprising the way drove off."

"Maybe there was an emergency."

Sophia nodded, deep in thought.

Something was definitely wrong.

Sophia was worried. Ethan had said he would text her around three and that was over an hour ago. The way he left in a hurry suggested maybe there was an emergency, but how would she know? She'd even texted him over an hour ago and never heard back.

"You're pacing," Chelsea said, looking through the refrigerator. "We need to figure out what to eat tonight for dinner. I'm already getting hungry."

"I'm not." Sophia went to the window and looked out again. "What if something happened to him? God, I don't like this feeling. Chelsea, I care about him. A lot."

Chelsea walked over from the kitchen and put her arm around Sophia. "Quit worrying so much."

"I can't help it. Is this what spouses of firefighters, police officers, and military go through every time their partner is late or doesn't call when they are supposed to?"

"I have no idea."

Sophia texted Ethan again and waited for a response. Nothing.

"Can you get me some phone numbers?" Sophia asked.

"Which ones?"

"South Tahoe Action team, police department, fire department, city hall, the local hospitals, Department of Forestry."

"Okay, you're freaking me out a little. He could be having a beer with some friends and you are thinking the worst possible things."

Chelsea was right, but Sophia couldn't control it. She saw the way he left. Something was wrong.

"I'll do it myself then," Sophia said. She grabbed her cell phone and searched on Google for as many places as possible to call. Somebody had to know something.

Then she stopped and looked up at Chelsea. "Wait a minute. You have Mike's number, right? Call him. He'll know for sure. He's Ethan's best friend."

Chelsea grabbed her phone. "If I find out Ethan is out grocery shopping or getting a manicure you are going to feel pretty ridiculous."

"I'm willing to take that chance."

Chelsea let out a deep sigh and dialed Mike. "Hey Mike, it's Chelsea." She stood and walked to the window, looking out. "I'm great, thank you. But my sister is worried about Ethan. She saw him take off in a hurry and he was supposed to text her. Do you know if everything is okay with him?"

She nodded. "Uh-huh."

Sophia moved closer. "What did he say?"

Chelsea waved Sophia away and continued to listen. "Uh-huh." She nodded again. "Okay, thanks for letting me know. I'll relay the info and talk to you later."

Chelsea disconnected the call and set the phone down on the side table.

"Tell me!" Sophia said. "Something's wrong. What is it?"

Chelsea turned to Sophia. "Okay, don't freak out but there was an avalanche up on Heavenly Mountain and Ethan went to help. Some people were buried."

Sophia swallowed hard and found it very difficult to speak. "Is Ethan okay?"

"Mike doesn't know. He said Ethan should be fine because he was going to help and wasn't the one stuck in the avalanche, but . . ."

"But what?"

"He also said avalanche rescues can be dangerous because they can trigger more avalanches."

Sophia stared at her sister for a few seconds. "I have to go." Sophia ran toward the door and slid out of her slippers and into her boots. Then she grabbed her jacket and gloves.

"What? Where are you going?"

Sophia wrapped a scarf around her neck and pulled the beanie over her head, down over her ears. "To the mountain. I have to find him. I have to make sure he's okay."

Chelsea pointed out the window. "You can't go up there! Are you crazy? That's what the experts are for. And they probably have it all blocked off anyway, so you won't get far. It'll just be a waste of time and *you* will end up getting lost."

"I'm willing to take my chances."

Chapter Seventeen

Ninety minutes later, Sophia was freezing beyond belief. She'd bought a ticket for the gondola and rode it up past the observation deck where she and Ethan had had coffee, all the way to the top of the mountain. It was practically deserted up there because of the cold and wind, but she kept hiking and searching, only to come up empty.

Where was he? And why didn't anyone know about the avalanche? Sophia was shivering and not only losing light, but hope as well. It was obvious she needed to head back down. She looked around, a little confused.

Shit. Which way? And where is Ethan?

Her eyes stung, but not from the cold. She was crying. She wanted so desperately to find Ethan, but she was losing hope. How could she find him when the mountain was so big?

A volunteer with the Heavenly Ski Patrol pulled up on a snowmobile a few minutes later. "What are you doing wandering out here by yourself?"

Sophia was so cold she could barely answer. "Do you know where the avalanche is?"

"Around here we don't *look* for avalanches—we try to get

away from them. Get on the back. You need to head back down the mountain."

"I need to find Ethan."

"Who's Ethan?"

"A man I met. A good, honest, decent man."

"Okay," the man said, a look of confusion on his face. "When did you last see him?"

"Yesterday. At Heavenly Ice."

"The ice skating rink?"

She nodded.

"Okay, you need to hop on so we can get you out of here."

"I need to find Ethan!

More tears.

The man took a few steps toward Sophia. "Get on the snowmobile now, or I will pick you up and put you there."

She crossed her arms. "You're just as pushy as he is, you know that?" She got on the back of the snowmobile, not saying another word.

The man drove over to the gondola platform and pointed to it. "Head back down now. You're lucky I found you. Don't mess with Mother Nature."

She nodded.

Don't mess with Mother Nature.

Ethan's words.

Sophia headed back down the mountain on the gondola, thinking about how foolish she had been. She *had* messed with Mother Nature. Again.

People died out there all the time—she knew that. And not only had she had zero success in finding Ethan, she felt terrible physically. Frozen to the core. It looked like she would need another one of those therapeutic baths when she got back to the house.

She got off the gondola and walked back to the house, wiping her nose just about every ten seconds. She finally made it back into the house and Chelsea flipped out.

"I was worried sick about you!" Chelsea helped pull Sophia's jacket and scarf off. "You are crazy! How could you do that? You're my only sister and if I lose you, I'll die!" Chelsea's eyes filled. "You need to get into the bath. Now."

Sophia didn't answer and did what she was told. Yeah, that was a stupid move. And she still hadn't found out anything about Ethan, so it was all for nothing.

Sophia's body tingled when she was sitting in the warm water. The bath felt good, but she could tell her body was weak, still recovering from the cold temperature on the top of the mountain. She took cold medicine, hoping it would nip whatever she was feeling in the bud and she wrapped herself in two blankets on the couch.

Chelsea prepared a cup of tea for Sophia, but it wasn't long after that Sophia closed her eyes and fell asleep on the couch. The biggest surprise she got was when she woke up and saw it was light outside.

It was the next day.

She had slept through the night without waking up once. Her body needed it she guessed, but the problem was she felt worse than before. She was stuffed up completely, and it even felt like she had a temperature.

Crap.

Sophia got up and ran into Chelsea in front of the bathroom.

"How are you feeling?" Chelsea asked, worry on her face.

"Not good. Have you heard from Ethan?"

Chelsea nodded. "He's fine, but you're not." She blew out a sigh and put her hand on Sophia's forehead. "You've got a fever. Go to the bathroom, then lay back down. I'll bring you something else to take."

Sophia nodded and went to the bathroom. A few minutes later she was back on the couch under the blankets.

Chelsea entered the family room with a glass of water and couple of pills. "Take these and relax."

"Thanks." Sophia took the pills and handed the glass back to Chelsea and sat back up. "Where is he? What happened? Is he really okay?"

"He's one hundred percent fine. He was here, actually. If you hadn't been such a zombie last night you would have —"

"Wait!" She winced and massaged her temples. "Remind me not to yell anymore, because that *really* hurts. Anyway, go back. What do you mean he was here? Like in this house?"

"Oh, yeah. He stopped by after Mike told him you were worried about him. He knelt down right before you there on the couch. Even kissed you on the forehead. Then he said he was so upset with you he'd kill you when you woke up. I guess I should let him know it's time for you to die."

"He kissed me on the forehead?"

Chelsea nodded and smiled. "Sure did."

"And I missed it?"

"It was sweet. He even made sure your feet were tucked in well so they didn't get cold. It's amazing the way he looked at you. He's hooked, no doubt."

"But I looked like shit last night!" She buried her head in the pillow.

Chelsea laughed. "You sure did, but lucky for you he didn't seem to care one bit. If he did, he wouldn't be coming back over today."

Sophia sat up. "What are you talking about? When is he coming back over?"

"Around lunchtime. He said he was bringing something special over for you."

She tried to stand and wobbled before collapsing back to the couch. "I need to shower and change and spray some Coco Chanel all over. And I need to do that right now."

Chelsea pushed her back down. "*You* need to rest. Do you want to get pneumonia?"

Sophia shook her head. But she also didn't want to look

like a complete disaster in front of Ethan.

"Relax," Chelsea said, rubbing Sophia's arm. "He's already seen you at your worst. Plus, the way he looks at you, it's obvious you already stole his heart. You have nothing to worry about. Trust me."

Sophia wasn't going to discuss it any longer because she had the sudden urge to close her eyes again. Her body was sending her a message, loud and clear, and she needed to listen. She guessed it wasn't longer than thirty seconds before she fell back asleep.

Ethan prepared his special soup for Sophia, hoping it would turn out just as good as it did the last time he made it. He still couldn't believe what Sophia had done. Going up to the top of the mountain by herself near the end of the day was reckless and crazy. She didn't take his warning seriously. He wanted to give her the lecture of her life, but right now his only focus was to take care of her and make sure she didn't get worse.

He added the rice to the chicken soup and a special Thai spice that would add a healing kick to the soup. He covered it back up, lowered the heat, and changed his clothes.

Ten minutes later with the pot of soup in his hands he walked across the snow.

He tapped lightly on the door in case Sophia was sleeping.

A few seconds later Chelsea opened the door.

"Come on in," she whispered. "Sleeping Beauty is still sleeping."

He nodded and stepped inside, following Chelsea to the kitchen but not before peeking at Sophia along the way. She looked peaceful and comfortable, wrapped up in her blankets on the couch. Just where he had seen her last night.

He set the soup on the kitchen counter and kept his voice low. "How is she doing?"

Chelsea pulled a bowl out of the cupboard and then grabbed a soup ladle. "Hard to tell right now. She was a little weak earlier and had a fever."

He ground his teeth. "Why didn't she listen? That woman is so stubborn."

"She's always been that way, as long as I can remember."

"I can hear you talking about me," she called out from the other room. "Try saying something nice. That might speed up my recovery."

Ethan chuckled. "How's this? You're lucky I don't kill you!"

"That's not nice."

Ethan shook his head in disbelief. How could he want to kill someone and kiss her at the same time? That woman drove him crazy, but there was no other place he would rather be than there in her house.

Chelsea placed a ladle and a soup spoon on the counter. "Here you go."

"Thanks."

She pointed down the hallway. "I'll be in my room if you two need anything. Take your time. Stay as long as you want. Even if she gets crabby."

"I heard that!" Sophia yelled out.

He scooped four ladlefuls of the soup into the bowl and headed to the family room where Sophia was sitting up, waiting for him.

He placed the bowl and spoon on the coffee table and sat next to her. "How are you feeling?"

"Embarrassed."

"Not mentally. How are you feeling physically?"

She crinkled her nose. "Like crap."

"Not a surprise," Ethan said. "I guess you noticed it can get cold out there."

"As much as I deserve one, please spare me the lecture. I'm not up for it right now."

"Fair enough. So I guess Chelsea told you I wanted to kill you then?"

She nodded. "And I don't blame you. Go ahead. Choose your weapon."

Ethan leaned over and kissed her on the lips. "I come in peace."

She blinked twice. "I would ask you to do that again, a few times, but I'm sure my breath smells like a junkyard.

211

Plus, I look like hell."

"Let me disagree with you."

She stared at him in disbelief.

"You look more like death," he added.

Sophia reached to her side, grabbed the pillow, and swatted Ethan on the head with it. "*That* is not nice."

He laughed. "What? You wanted me to be *real*, remember?"

"Not *that* real!"

He leaned over and kissed her on the lips again.

"Stop doing that!" She sneezed. "See? You're going to get sick."

"Superman doesn't get sick, so don't you worry about me. I've had my flu shot for the season, if that's what you have. Now I need to make sure you get better, so I brought you some soup."

"I hate soup."

"Look, I don't make a lot of things, but this is something I'm proud of."

Sophia fiddled with the blanket. "Sorry."

"Even when you're weak, you're still stubborn. And you may *hate* soup, but I don't think you will hate *my* soup. It's the tastiest soup in all the land, and it has magical powers. You'll be back on your feet in no time."

She glanced over at the bowl on the coffee table. "Really. Believe me. Don't take it personally. I hate soup."

"I. Don't. Care. You're eating it. It will make you feel

better." He reached over and grabbed the bowl, then lifted a spoonful toward her mouth.

"Not going to happen."

"Yes, it is, Lady Stubborn. Open!"

She gave him the evil eye and then finally opened her mouth.

He grinned and inserted the spoon in her mouth, then pulled it out when he was sure it was empty.

Sophia looked up at Ethan. "You made this?" She chewed and nodded. "What's in that? Is it Chinese or Thai?"

Just the fact she wasn't complaining about it anymore was a good sign. She didn't say she hated it. Now he hoped she would eat the entire bowl because he was confident it would make her feel better.

"Your taste buds are working, that's good. And you're right—it's Thai soup. Chicken, rice, and a special ingredient I cannot reveal."

"I taste coconut and mint and something else."

"Very good. Have a little more." He grabbed another spoonful and held it close to her mouth.

She took the spoon from his hand. "I don't need your help."

"I should know this by now. Stubborn."

"Pushy." She ate another spoonful and then grabbed the bowl from him, eating the entire thing in two minutes.

Ethan took the empty bowl and spoon from her and placed it back on the table. Then he grinned, not saying a word. He was happy she finished it and it felt good to take care of someone. It felt good to take care of Sophia.

"Wipe that cocky grin off your face," she said.

Ethan touched his face with his hand, then squeezed his cheeks a few times. "Was that cocky? Oh, I'm *so* sorry about that." He peeked under the blanket at her feet. "Cute socks for your tiny size seven feet."

She reached down and covered her feet back up. "Don't make fun of my feet."

"Who's making fun?" He reached under the blanket and grabbed a foot, massaging it. "I said they were cute."

"Why are you doing all this?"

"Here we go again. You have a problem with me being nice again? Think I'm up to no good, right? Soon you'll fall into my trap and I'll have you right where I want you."

She didn't respond.

"Why can't you enjoy it? Please. Close your eyes and lean back."

She gave him a skeptical look.

"Do it."

"Pushy."

"Stubborn."

Sophia hesitated and then closed her eyes, leaning her head back.

He massaged the center of the big toe on her left foot, then the bottom of her big toe, the instep, the sole, the heel, and finally each toe individually. Then he switched over to the right foot and repeated the process.

Her bottom lip curled up and she sighed again.

"I take it by your expression you're enjoying this?"

She opened her eyes for a second and pointed to her feet. "I need a little less talk and a lot more action." She closed her eyes.

He chuckled. "It would be a pleasure. I have to get you better for New Year's Eve."

She opened her eyes again. "What's happening on New Year's Eve?"

He grinned. "You'll find out soon enough."

Chapter Eighteen

New Year's Eve had arrived and Sophia couldn't wait to celebrate with Ethan. He had been amazing the last few days, nursing her back to health with a different soup each day. She had to admit being sick and eating soup had never been so fun.

Every day he brought the soup and every day she told him she hated soup. Yes, they bickered like they always had, and it was almost becoming expected. Her grandparents bickered for fifty years and they were inseparable, so she didn't always think it was such a bad thing. Sophia felt something special for the ski instructor next door. *Very* special.

She was falling in love with Ethan.

Ethan had accomplished something that not even Chelsea was able to do. He had convinced Sophia to turn off her phone for the last forty-eight hours of the year so she could disconnect and enjoy the last part of her vacation. It wasn't easy to do, since the phone had always been her lifeline to Hollywood, but she did it anyway. Just for him.

The good news was Chelsea and Mike would join them at the party, since Uncle Al had volunteered to watch Violet and Bear for the evening. He'd said all he needed to be happy was a six-pack of wine coolers and an HD television to watch the ball drop in Time's Square.

Ethan had surprised Sophia with tickets to the New Year's Eve event at the Heavenly Ballroom just down the street. The party was typically attended by mostly locals and included dinner, cocktails, dancing to a DJ, party favors, and a champagne toast at midnight. Sophia anticipated it would be a wonderful evening, and she couldn't wait to get the party started.

"You almost ready?" Chelsea yelled from the other room. "They will be here any minute."

"Ready!" Sophia called back, checking out her long black dress in the bathroom mirror. Ethan had recommended a local women's boutique and both Sophia and Chelsea found dresses and matching shoes.

Chelsea popped her head in the bedroom, and her mouth dropped open. "Wow, sis. You look even more gorgeous than you did in the store. You're going to give Ethan whiplash with that thing."

Sophia laughed. "I hope not. He needs to dance tonight."

"Seriously . . . that man will get down on his knees and beg you to marry him after he sees you!"

"Whoa, whoa, whoa. Slow down there. We're going out on New Year's Eve. It's a date and chance to go out, have fun, and celebrate. There are still details to be worked out and things to be discussed before there is *any* talk of something serious and long term."

"Well, you can pretend all you want, but I can see what's happening with my own two eyes. The same thing is happening to me and Mike and I'd say *yes* if he asked me to marry him."

"That's a little impulsive. The ink is not even dry on your divorce papers and you'd do that?"

"Mike can ask me to do *anything* at all and I'd say yes."

"You're so easy!"

"I know! Isn't it wonderful?"

Sophia looked over Chelsea's shoulder. "The door's not open, is it? Do you think they would walk in and eavesdrop on our conversation? I thought I heard something, like movement."

Chelsea stared at Sophia for a beat, then disappeared down the hallway. A few seconds later she returned and held up her fist. "Do you want to get hurt? You scared the crap out of me!"

Sophia laughed. "I thought I heard something! Anyway, enough of this talk. We have secrets and they need to stay that way. Did I tell you that you look amazing?"

"You did, but I don't mind hearing it again."

"You look amazing."

Chelsea did a curtsy. "*Thank* you."

Her burgundy dress brought out her sparkling eyes, making her look like another celebrity. Chelsea knew how to do her makeup even better than Sophia, who had someone doing it for her most of the time.

Mike and Ethan arrived a few minutes later and stepped inside. They both wore black pinstripe suits with black leather shoes. The only difference was Ethan had a turquoise tie while Mike's was a gold and blue paisley tie.

Ethan was handsome as hell.

Sophia had gotten so used to seeing him in jeans and ski gear that the formal wear was a shock to her system.

The man looked irresistible.

The best part was, Ethan was scoring serious points by the way he was looking at her.

He stepped closer to Sophia and kissed her on the cheek. He eyed her from head to toe and shook his head. "How am I supposed to focus on food, or dancing, or walking when you're wearing something like that?"

She smiled. "I guess you'll just have to figure that out."

"I guess I will. Without a doubt you'll be the most beautiful woman at the party."

Mike cleared his throat. "I will have to disagree with you there, Ethan." He stepped closer to Chelsea and kissed her on the cheek. "*Chelsea* will be the most beautiful woman at the party."

"Impossible," Ethan said. "Sophia wins."

"Chelsea wins."

A horn honked outside.

Sophia held up her hand. "We're *both* flattered and

impressed with your enthusiasm, but is it possible to continue this conversation in the taxi? I want to celebrate!"

Ethan chuckled. "You heard the woman. Let's go. And don't argue with her because she's stubborn as hell and will win the argument."

The Heavenly Ballroom was elegant and festive, the tables dressed with gold linens and topped with red candles. Strings of white lights hung from the ceiling and met in the middle, connecting to a giant LED cube that was counting down to midnight on all four sides. Every corner of the ballroom had a ten-foot Christmas tree, decorated with colorful lights and ornaments.

Ethan, Sophia, Mike, and Chelsea had already enjoyed appetizers and were now seated at their assigned table, finishing up a delicious prime rib and baked potato dinner. Then New York cheesecake and coffee were served.

Mike took a bite of cheesecake and nodded his approval. "This is the life, I'll tell ya. Bringing in the new year with good food, my best friend, and two amazing women. I could get used to this."

Chelsea smiled and cuddled against Mike. "Me, too."

"Now if we can just get these beautiful ladies to move here, we would be set for life." Mike added a wink.

That sounded wonderful, but Sophia knew it was easier said than done and it wasn't something she wanted to discuss at the party.

"Why don't we enjoy the moment and take one day at a

time?" Ethan asked, looking over at Sophia.

He had read her mind.

"I'm with you," Chelsea said.

The DJ started up the music and Sophia took that as her cue to bail from the conversation. She jumped up from her seat and turned to Ethan. "Time to dance!"

Ethan stood. "Sounds good." He grabbed her hand and led her to the dance floor. A few seconds later Mike and Chelsea were dancing next to them. And they danced the night away, the time getting closer and closer to midnight.

Sophia couldn't remember the last time she went dancing. The last time she celebrated New Year's Eve in public. The last time she had so much fun and felt so cherished and pampered.

Finally the moment came, the countdown to midnight.

Champagne was poured and everyone in the room gathered on the dance floor underneath the LED counter as the DJ helped them count down from ten to one, followed by the screams of "Happy New Year!"

The DJ played "Auld Lang Syne" by Guy Lombardo. The guests hugged, kissed, and sang along to the song.

Ethan grabbed Sophia by the waist and pulled her close. "Happy New Year."

Sophia caressed the side of his cheek and said, "Happy New Year."

And then they kissed. A kiss to bring in the new year and to take their relationship to a deeper place, a more meaningful level.

Sophia was happy, and nervous, and hopeful.

Being in Ethan's arms felt like home and she wanted to tell him how she felt.

Ethan and Mike walked Sophia and Chelsea across the path toward their front door. The night was coming to an end and it couldn't have been better for Sophia. Or at least that's what she thought until snowflakes began to fall.

"Snow!" Sophia said, holding her palms out in front of her. "I *love* it!" She looked up and reached her arms to the sky, spinning around and enjoying every snowflake that hit her face, her hair, her mouth. "This is magical."

"See what you've been missing all these years?" Chelsea said. "But I think that's enough. It's cold out here and we don't want you to have a relapse."

"Fine." Sophia turned to Ethan and squeezed his arm. "She's almost as pushy as you."

"Wait," Mike said. "There's a problem."

"What?" Ethan said.

Mike shrugged. "We're all walking to the front porch to say good night and . . . I don't know about *you*, but I plan on giving Chelsea one hell of a kiss before I go."

"I had planned on kissing Sophia instead."

The girls laughed.

"Not funny," Mike said. "My point is, I don't want to kiss Chelsea while you're kissing Sophia *right* next to us. That would be weird and I would like to have a little *privacy*."

"Well, *excuse* us."

"I have an idea," Sophia chimed in. "You two go ahead. Ethan and I will stay right here for another minute."

"That woman is smart," Mike said. "She's a keeper."

Chelsea held up a finger. "Only one minute. I don't want you getting sick again."

Mike wrapped his arm around Chelsea's shoulder and continued to the house.

Ethan turned to Sophia. "You're going to get sick again."

She placed a finger against his lips. "Don't start." She stared up into the night sky as the snowflakes continued to lightly fall on her face.

It reminded her of *Bridget Jones's Diary* again, when Mr. Darcy kissed Bridget in the snow. So romantic. In fact . . .

"Kiss me right here," Sophia said, looking into Ethan's eyes. "Kiss me in the snow."

Ethan's eyes grew wide. "I don't have a problem with that at all."

He pulled her body tightly against his and kissed her.

And it was magical. Just like in the movie.

No. Better. This was real.

"Okay," Chelsea yelled from the front porch. "Get your butt in the house now!"

Sophia and Ethan said their goodbyes and agreed to chat in the morning.

Once inside the house, Sophia closed the front door and smiled. "What a night."

Chelsea nodded. "Yeah. It's going to be a great year. I can feel it."

"Me, too." Sophia hugged Chelsea. "I'm beat and going to bed. We'll talk in the morning."

"Sounds good."

"I'm happy for you, sis."

"I'm happy for you, too."

Sophia brushed her teeth, put on her pajamas and slid into bed.

She had had the best New Year's Eve, and it was all because of Ethan.

"Oh, crap," she mumbled to herself, realizing she never thanked him. She told him she had a wonderful time, but that was it. No thank you.

Sophia shook her head in disgust and grabbed her phone from the bedside table, turning it on. She would just send Ethan a quick thank you text, then go to bed. It had been a long, wonderful day, but she was tired.

The phone powered up and vibrated six or seven times after she tapped in her passcode.

"Oh, my God!" Sophia practically screamed, scrolling through the phone.

A few seconds later Chelsea entered Sophia's bedroom

in her pajamas. "What's wrong? *Why* are you on your phone now? Turn that thing off and go to sleep."

"I was going to send Ethan a quick text and saw all these missed calls from Brad." Sophia tapped a few icons on the phone. "Text messages, too. Some from today, some from yesterday. His text messages have a lot of exclamation points like he's yelling at me. He says to check my voicemail and call him back ASAP. Hang on . . ."

She tapped the voicemail icon and listened to the message from Brad.

"Sophia! How come you're not answering your phone or responding to my text messages? You're running out of time if you want this part. They've made the offer. This is it, the big one. Can you say *Oscar*? But seriously, they need to know now and they want to meet on January 2nd! Call me."

Sophia stared at her phone, deep in thought.

And the Academy Award for actress in a leading role goes to . . ." Tom Hanks smiled and slid his index finger under the flap of the envelope to open it, pulling out the card. "Sophia Harris!"

"What is it?" Chelsea asked, sitting on the side of the bed. She rubbed Sophia on the side of the arm. "What's going on? Did someone die?"

"No. Someone is about to be reborn."

Chelsea tilted her head to the side. "What are you talking about?"

Sophia set the phone back on the bedside table. "I've been offered a role that is guaranteed to get me the Oscar nomination. Vacation is over. I need to go back home."

"What?" Chelsea practically yelled. She jumped off the bed and turned around, hands on her hips. "We're not cutting our vacation short! We're having lunch at Mike's tomorrow. I've never been to his place. It's New Year's Day, the first meal of the year. You can't leave."

"I have to."

"No. You. Don't. You make the decisions. This is *your* life. And what about Ethan? You love him—don't deny it. You're just going to pack up and leave him? Just like that?"

"The Academy Award has been my dream! You know how much it means to me, how much it would mean to my career. Now I have the opportunity and there is no way I am going to pass it up."

Chelsea shook her head. "You think that award will make you happy?"

"Yes. I do."

"It's just an award," Chelsea said, letting out a deep breath. "If you think that's all it takes for you to be happy, you're *so* wrong. What about the happiness you've been experiencing here? What about Ethan?"

Sophia didn't want to be having this conversation with her sister at almost two in the morning. Chelsea didn't understand.

"If *this* is what you've been waiting for, and if this is the best news ever, why aren't you jumping up and down with joy? Why aren't you smiling? Why don't you look happy?"

Sophia didn't answer.

"That's what I thought," Chelsea said, shaking her head and walking toward the door. "We can talk about this in the morning when we're both fresh." She stopped at the door and turned back around. "I love you, Sophia. You know that. But sometimes you just don't know what's good for you. Sometimes it's sitting right in front of your face and you can't even see it. And that makes me sad."

Chapter Nineteen

Ethan couldn't remember the last time he'd woken up on New Year's Day with so much energy. It was only eight in the morning and he felt fresh and alive, like he was ready to run a marathon. He'd already taken down the Christmas tree, boxed it up, and stuck it back in the garage rafters, along with all the decorations. He already vacuumed the entire house, too. Surprising, considering he'd barely slept four hours. He'd have left the tree one more day, but since New Year's Day lunch would be at Mike's, nobody would be there to enjoy it.

He knew his abundance of positive energy and adrenaline had everything to do with lovely Sophia. New Year's Eve with her was amazing. He knew before last night he was falling in love with her, but now it was official.

Ethan loved Sophia.

He loved her and would scream it to the world. Well, maybe not at the moment. It was still early for some people. Who knew how long it would be until Sophia woke up? She had complained about their early start that morning he took her to the ice skating rink, so it would be best to let her sleep.

Ethan grabbed the leash and jingled it. "Let's go, Bear.

This is the perfect morning for a walk."

The snowstorm had passed and there was nothing but blue skies. After the walk, maybe he would clean the bathrooms or his car. Ethan chuckled, thinking about how much energy he had.

He took Bear on a loop around Wonderland Lane, past Heavenly Resort, stopping in an area where his dog preferred pooping only when it was sunny for some odd reason.

Ethan pulled on Bear's leash when he got back to the bottom of his street to grab the ringing phone from his pocket. It was Mike.

"This is a surprise," Ethan said. "I can't believe you're up already."

"Gotta work, you know that," Mike said. "I'm on my way to clear a few driveways, but many of my regular customers are out of town this week, which is great. More time to prepare lunch. Violet is very excited to have the girls over. I want to spend every minute with Chelsea before she heads back to Beverly Hills."

"Then what?"

Mike and Ethan hadn't had time to talk much the last couple of days and Ethan was curious if he and Chelsea had had a talk about taking their relationship to the next level. Obviously that would involve one of them moving, which most likely would have to be Chelsea since Mike had two businesses in Lake Tahoe.

"We briefly chatted about it," Mike said. "We both agreed that a long distance relationship wouldn't work, unless it's temporary. One of us would have to make the move if we wanted things to continue, which we both do."

"And?"

Mike chuckled. "Well, believe or not, she says she wants to move here ASAP."

Ethan stopped walking. "This is amazing."

"Tell me about it. What about you and Sophia?"

That was the big question.

Ethan and Sophia would need to discuss it soon. He had no interest in moving to Los Angeles. He loved the slower life and beauty of Lake Tahoe. He loved being a ski instructor and volunteering with the South Tahoe Action Team.

"I don't know," Ethan answered. "Would Sophia be willing to give up her celebrity lifestyle and move here? Seems like a lot to ask from someone with her status and her type of career."

"Most people would do anything for love," Mike said.

Ethan rounded the corner of his street, almost home. He was four houses from his place when he spotted a yellow taxi with the trunk open next door. Just the sight of the taxi freaked Ethan out. "Mike, let me call you right back."

"You got it."

Ethan slipped the phone in his pocket and watched as the taxi driver threw a large suitcase in in the trunk. A few seconds later Sophia walked down the driveway and got in the backseat. Ethan picked up the pace as the driver closed the trunk, got in the car, and started the engine.

What's going on? Where is Sophia going?

The car took off, coming in Ethan's direction.

Ethan waved his free arm at the taxi. "Stop!"

Bear pulled toward the taxi and the driver slammed on the brakes.

Ethan locked eyes with Sophia in the backseat.

"What are you doing?" Ethan asked. "What about us?"

Sophia had a blank look on her face. No emotion. She didn't lower the window. She shook her head no and then looked away as the driver maneuvered around him.

Ethan stood there in the middle of the street.

Devastated.

The taxi disappeared from sight.

What was going on? What happened? Had he done something wrong?

"Ethan!" Chelsea yelled, from the porch of their house.

He rushed up the driveway and up the stairs to the porch.

Chelsea stood there, crying. "I'm sorry, Ethan. I'm so sorry. You don't deserve this."

Ethan's heart was in his stomach. Had the woman of his dreams just abandoned him?

"I don't get it," Ethan said, barely having the energy to speak the words. "What happened? What did I do wrong?" Bear reached up to lick Chelsea's hand. "Not now, Bear."

Chelsea shook her head, tears streaming down her face. "You did nothing wrong. My sister is a fool. I'm so pissed off at her, you have no idea."

Ethan didn't understand what was happening. One moment he was on top of the world and the next, his life was sliding toward hell.

"Why?" Ethan asked. "We had the most amazing night last night. This whole week. I don't get it."

Chelsea sniffled and wiped. "She's been obsessed with winning the Academy Award for a while, but they didn't offer her the right roles until now. Sophia was offered the role of a lifetime as she called it. She accepted it and that's why she left."

"Okay . . ." He ran his fingers through his hair, trying to think. Something didn't make sense. "But why would she leave without saying goodbye? Without us chatting about where we stand?"

"Because seeing you would have changed her mind, and she didn't want to change her mind."

"But . . . I love her, Chelsea. I love your sister and I was going to tell her today."

"And she loves you too—I'm sure of it. We got in a big fight this morning because she said there was nothing more important than that movie role. She was lying to herself."

Nothing more important than that movie role.

The words burned like acid in his stomach.

Ethan nodded, now knowing where he stood in her life.

He didn't mean enough to Sophia. Didn't mean anything at all, most likely. Chelsea said her sister loved him, but he didn't believe it. No way.

That wasn't how you showed someone you loved them.

Four years ago, Ethan was left with a broken heart when his girlfriend jumped into an actor's bed. Funny how things in life seemed to repeat themselves.

Hollywood broke his heart.

Again.

Chapter Twenty

Ethan entered his house and removed the leash from Bear, dropping it on the floor. He didn't have the energy to hang it where it was supposed to go on the hook. He wasn't sure he would have the energy to do anything.

He felt shattered. Lost.

Lost without Sophia.

So lost Ethan didn't remember walking to the family room and sitting on Bear's couch.

Bear stared at him, a look of confusion on the dog's face.

Ethan pushed down twice on the couch with the palm of his hand. "You're spoiled, you know? Your couch is much better than my couch."

Bear probably wondered what the hell was wrong with his dad. He hopped up on the couch, plopping down against Ethan's leg.

Ethan reached to his side and stroked Bear along his thick, fluffy coat. "Life sucks, Bear."

Bear just stared at him.

"You've got it easy, but let me give you some advice. Stay away from women because you don't ever want to feel the way I'm feeling right now."

Bear dropped his head down and closed his eyes.

"Yeah, I don't blame you for ignoring me."

Ethan was going crazy, having a one-sided conversation with his dog.

He massaged his temples and blew out a deep breath, wondering how long the pain would last.

Ethan thought he had been living the dream before he had met Sophia, but he couldn't have been more wrong. The dream had started *after* he had met her. Then the dream turned into a nightmare. The best thing that had happened to him in years had left without a word.

Ethan jumped to his feet at the sound of a car door outside, suddenly feeling hopeful and energetic. Sophia must have returned. She'd realized it was insane to end such a good thing. They were meant to be together. Forever.

He swung the front door open, ran to the edge of the deck, and peered over the edge.

The energy was sucked out of his body again.

It was Mike.

Ethan sighed and stared out into the forest. The snow didn't seem so white. The pine trees didn't seem so green. The air didn't seem so fresh. As hard as it was to comprehend, Lake Tahoe wasn't as beautiful without Sophia there. It had lost its magic.

Mike came up the stairs and pointed back to his snow plow. "I only have a couple of minutes. I have a few more driveways to clear, but Chelsea just called and told me what happened."

Mike gave him a hug and Ethan had to muster every bit of strength in his body to not break down and cry in front of his best friend.

"Woof!"

Ethan gestured for Mike to come in as Bear greeted him at the door.

They headed to the kitchen in silence and Ethan turned to face him. "You want a cup of coffee or something?"

Mike shook his head. "I'm good. I have a thermos in the truck."

Ethan jammed his hands in his pockets, not sure what to say.

Mike squeezed his shoulder. "I'm so sorry."

"I'll get over it."

"Will you?"

"I have to," Ethan replied. "Life goes on. She doesn't want me and I have to accept that."

Mike leaned against the kitchen island, deep in thought. "This is all my fault."

"How?"

"I encouraged you to go for it. I thought she was different, really. I thought she was good for you."

Ethan nodded. "Me, too."

How was he going to be okay without Sophia close by? Without her smile that warmed up the room? He needed to figure out how to live without thinking about her or missing her every minute. His heart was broken and it felt impossible to go back to his old life.

"Have you tried calling her? Seeing if you can talk it through?"

"You know I've never been one to force anything. It has to happen naturally. Besides, we could get back together again tomorrow, only to have the same thing happen next year or the year after that. Then what happens when the next *role of a lifetime* comes around? Her career is more important than everything else in her life and soon enough I'd be tossed to the side again. Yeah. This was the best thing that could have happened."

Mike raised an eyebrow, looking skeptical. "Do you *really* believe that?"

Ethan shrugged. "I have to."

Sophia stared out the jet window at the beautiful snow-capped mountains as they flew out of Lake Tahoe Airport. Who knew if she would ever see it again, but that was something she shouldn't be thinking about. She'd decided to head back to LA and now she would have to live with it. She would also have to live with the guilt that was consuming her entire body, right down to her core.

How could she have left without saying goodbye to Ethan? Without at least giving him an explanation of what she was doing and *why* she was doing it?

She knew exactly why.

Because just looking into Ethan's eyes and feeling his touch would change her mind instantly, and she didn't want to be weak. Ethan had too much power over her and she couldn't take the risk. That's why she felt like a coward.

It had torn her apart to see the pain and confusion in his eyes.

She felt like a coward treating Ethan that way. He'd been nothing but kind since the first day she'd met him on the side of the road, and he deserved better.

That didn't change the fact that she was making the right decision. This was an opportunity no actor in her right mind would pass up. How many people could say they were nominated for the industry's most prestigious award, let alone win it? She wanted it. She had wanted it badly for a long time and Ethan just wouldn't understand.

Still, she would miss Ethan, she couldn't lie to herself. His smile. His touch. His kisses. Even when he was being pushy. He was an amazing person and deserved someone to love forever. It wouldn't be Sophia.

Two hours later Sophia was back inside her home in Beverly Hills. She walked through the mansion, every step of her heels echoing off the walls.

She stopped and looked around, wondering why she had such a big place. It suddenly felt cold. Not cold like Lake Tahoe, but cold like the inside of her heart. It wasn't a home to her, if that made sense. More like an object.

The ring of her cell phone distracted her from the odd sensation.

It was Chelsea.

Sophia was in no mood to argue with her sister, but the two had made a pact many years ago. They agreed to always stick together through the highs and lows and *never* avoid the other when they were having their differences. She loved Chelsea with all her heart and wouldn't go back on her word now or ever as tempted as she might be.

"Hi."

"Hey there. You made it back okay."

"Yeah . . ."

Silence.

Not a surprise. That was one of the biggest fights they'd ever had.

"I love you," Chelsea said.

The sentiment surprised Sophia. She knew her sister loved her but she was sure Chelsea was calling to convince her to go back to Lake Tahoe or to tell her how devastated Ethan was and make her feel even more guilty.

"I love you, too."

Chelsea sighed into the phone. "Are you sure you know what you're doing? I think you're making a huge mistake."

"Only time will tell. And if it *is* a mistake, then I guess I'll learn from it, right?"

"Most likely, but by then it'll probably be too late."

"Too late for what?"

"Too late for Ethan."

Sophia didn't know how to respond to that and maybe it was best she didn't. She slid the patio door open and walked into the backyard. After kicking off her shoes, she stepped onto the first step of the swimming pool, just like Chelsea did whenever she came over.

The palm trees were swaying in the wind and it felt like it was almost eighty degrees outside—crazy, considering it was the beginning of January.

Funny how Sophia longed for the snow, like she hadn't been there in ages. Or most likely that longing was for Ethan. She squashed those thoughts immediately. No need to torture herself. She'd made her decision and had to stick to it.

"Anyway . . ." Chelsea said. "It doesn't sound like you're in the mood to talk, so I'll let you go. I'm going to stay a few more days if that's okay with you. I'm having lunch with Mike and Violet, but Ethan won't be coming. The reason is obvious."

She decided to ignore that last remark. "Of course that's okay. Stay as long as you like. Let me know when you're ready to come back and I'll see if the jet is available. If not, you'll have to fly a commercial flight out of Reno, but I can buy you a ticket online."

"That's not necessary," Chelsea said.

"Hey, you know I like to help."

"Sophia, *you're* the one who needs help right now."

Ouch.

That hurt.

Sophia said goodbye to Chelsea and went back inside to unpack her suitcase. The first thing she pulled out was the elegant black dress she had worn for the New Year's party. She held it up against her body, looking in the mirror. It was a beautiful dress. Then she smelled it. Ethan's cologne was still there, mixed with her perfume.

The look on Ethan's face when he came to pick her up was unforgettable. She loved the way he looked at her. The way he touched her.

She had to admit she was surprised Ethan hadn't called or texted after she sped away in the taxi. The men in Hollywood never gave up so easily.

Ethan was different though. He liked things to happen naturally or not at all.

As for what he said on the street . . .

What about us?

Those words were heartbreaking.

And she was sure she would remember them for the rest of her life.

Chapter Twenty-One

Two weeks later . . .

Sophia rubbed the back of neck as her stomach churned. She tapped her fingernails on the kitchen counter a few times and then stuck one of them in her mouth, mangling it with her teeth. She continued to chew on one of her nails, deep in thought.

"You want fries with that?" Chelsea asked from her bar stool on the other side of the island. "Seriously, you look like you belong in a straitjacket."

"I think that would help. Do you have one?"

"I'll get you one for your birthday. Take a deep breath. Everything will be fine, you'll see."

Sophia hoped so.

An hour earlier she'd decided to fly back to Lake Tahoe to tell Ethan she couldn't live without him. She wasn't sure how he'd respond because two weeks was a long time.

"Maybe he's married now with children," Sophia said, fully aware what she had said was completely ridiculous.

Chelsea laughed. "Right. After two weeks. Okay, I'll call the crazy house and see if they have room for you."

Kiss Me in the Snow

The last couple of weeks had been pure torture for Sophia. She'd had meetings with her agent and publicist, as well as the director, producers, and actors of her next project. She was a complete zombie in every meeting. Half of them she didn't even remember. She couldn't focus, she couldn't sleep, she couldn't function, really.

Sophia was a complete mess.

She was supposed to be happy, but someone forgot to send her the memo to let her know happiness was only possible if she had Ethan in her life.

That's when she'd decided she'd had enough and had to do something about it.

Sophia quit the movie she was working on. Just like that.

Brad warned her there could be repercussions and a possible lawsuit from the movie studio.

Sophia had bigger things to worry about—like losing the man who she couldn't get out of her mind, no matter how hard she tried.

Just to be on the safe side, she'd called Hilary Swank and Anne Hathaway. She'd told them the role would be available and to call their agents immediately if they were interested.

"You're pacing again," Chelsea said. "Stop it or I'll tie you to one of the palm trees in the back. Why are you so nervous, anyway?"

"I don't know, I just am."

Chelsea got up from the bar stool and circled around the kitchen island to hug her sister. "Relax. Everything will be fine. Look how it all turned out for me and Mike."

"That's because one of you didn't pack up and leave the other in the middle of the night."

"You left in the morning."

"You know what I mean."

Sophia couldn't be happier for her sister. Chelsea would move to Lake Tahoe soon to be with Mike and Violet. Sophia would be open to the same move, but that depended on how receptive Ethan was to the idea, and if he didn't despise her completely.

She'd soon find out.

Later that afternoon, the driver stopped in front of Ethan's house and glanced at Sophia in the rearview mirror. "I'll be at the Denny's restaurant down the way. Just send me a text with the status."

"Will do. Thanks."

Sophia took a deep breath and made her way up his stairs. She glanced over at the spot where Ethan had kissed her in the snow and hoped that wasn't the last time she would get one of those.

Sophia stopped in front of the door, took another deep breath, and rang the doorbell.

"Woof!"

Ethan opened the door a few seconds later and froze. "Oh . . ." He glanced down at her purse, then lifted his gaze again to meet hers. "Hello."

"Hi."

Ethan finally opened the door a little farther. "Come in." He wasn't smiling.

"Thanks."

Her reception from Ethan was cold. No hug. No kiss. Not emotion. She shouldn't be surprised considering the way she had left him.

She petted Bear on the head and the dog gave her hand a lick.

At least someone was happy to see her.

She followed Ethan into the kitchen, no words spoken between them.

Ethan opened the refrigerator. "Something to drink? I'm going to have a beer."

"No. Thank you."

He popped the top of the beer and took a sip, waiting for her to speak.

This was it.

"You must be wondering why I'm here."

"It crossed my mind, yes."

She nodded and figured she would just put it out there. "First, I want to say I'm sorry for the way I left. It was wrong and I regret it."

He avoided eye contact and took another pull of his beer. "That's okay."

"It's not okay. You don't deserve that. And can you please look at me for just a moment?"

He hesitated and then locked eyes with her.

Sophia stepped closer. "I came back here to see if there was still a chance we could see each other. A chance to be together and start over."

Ethan set his beer on the kitchen counter. "I think it's obvious there's no possibility of this working out. I mean, look at us. We live in two different worlds. I lead a simple life and I have no plans of changing that. Lake Tahoe and Beverly Hills are complete opposites. My world is filled with pinecones and bears and ski slopes and *your world* is filled with Gucci and glitz and glamour."

"But that's not me . . . the Gucci, the glitz, and the glamour. That's not me at all."

He furled his eyebrows together. "You're telling me you don't have a Gucci bag in your closet at home?"

Shit.

She couldn't lie to him. She didn't want to have Ethan back in her life based on a lie.

"Okay," Sophia said, swallowing hard. "I do have *one* Gucci bag. Okay, maybe two, but—"

"There you go." He took another sip of his beer. "That's your world. Much different than my world."

She stared at him for a moment. "You're telling me you don't want to see me anymore because I own a Gucci bag?"

"No. I'm telling you I don't want to see you again because my heart can't take another brutal beating." He shook his head, pain registering on his face. "And who's to say it won't happen again?"

"*I* say it won't happen again. I promise you that. Forget about my world and the Gucci bags; I'll give them away if you want. There are so many things in life just waiting for us. All we have to do is choose. I've chosen wrong in the past and for that I'm sorry. But I've learned from my mistakes." She grabbed his hands, an expectant look in her eyes. "I choose you."

Ethan hesitated and then pulled his hands from hers. "I can't, Sophia. I just can't."

Two hours later Ethan still hadn't moved from the couch. He just sat there. Numb. Turning down Sophia and watching her walk out that door was one of the hardest things he had ever done in his life. It took all his strength not to pull her in his arms and hold on forever. When she said she chose him, Ethan wanted to kiss her and let her back in his life, but that would have been the easy thing to do. His heart was broken into a thousand pieces and the pain was unbearable.

Ethan couldn't risk that happening again.

Still, he wondered if he had made the right decision.

Of course, I did.

He was happy before he met her and he could be happy again. Not as happy as he was when he was with her, but happy nonetheless. Okay, maybe *unworried* was a better word choice.

There was a knock at the front door.

"Woof!"

Ethan wasn't dumb enough to think Sophia had returned. He had no doubts she was on her way back to her LA.

He opened the door to Uncle Al, who zipped right by Ethan straight toward the kitchen

"Please come in," Ethan said to himself, closing the door.

By the time Ethan got the kitchen Uncle Al was already popping the top of a beer. "You really need to get wine coolers." He took a sip of the beer. "Where is she?"

"Who?"

"Sophia? She in the bathroom?"

"She's gone."

Uncle Al froze with the beer just an inch from his lips. "What do you mean *gone?*"

"I mean she's on her way back to LA."

"And you let her go? What kind of idiot is my nephew?"

"I don't need to hear this."

Uncle Al shook his head in disbelief. "Do you even *know* what she did?"

"You mean besides break my heart?"

"She *saved* the theater!"

Ethan just stared at Uncle Al, unable to form words. What the hell was he talking about?

"She donated a boatload of money to make it happen. I

mean an obscene amount with a lot of zeros. Because of her generosity, the theater and all of its programs will continue to run for years. And that means Violet can continue."

Ethan ran his hands through his hair. "Why didn't anyone tell me?"

"I just found out myself. Man, you really messed up letting that woman go. You need to have your head examined. Did you know there are over 1.7 million brain injuries every year? Must have happened to you."

The front door opened.

"Woof!"

Mike entered the kitchen, hands on his hips. "Why the hell did you let her go?"

"Well, hello to you, too," Ethan said. "Can we talk about football or something else, maybe?"

"Answer the man," Uncle Al chimed in. "Tell him why you're such an idiot."

Ethan set his beer down and crossed his arms. "So this is how it's going to go? Are you in this together, teaming up against me?"

"Damn straight," Uncle Al said, clinking Mike's bottle. "No need to beat around the bush."

"I made the right decision."

Uncle Al pointed at Ethan. "Did you know you can die of a broken heart? Literally *die*?"

Ethan held up his hand. "I really don't need to hear this now."

"Yes, you do. The blood pumping in and out of your heart becomes temporarily blocked by a shitload of stress hormones, which are secreted in response to someone telling you to get lost forever. Thousands of deaths have been reported."

Ethan took another sip of his beer. "Well then . . . please let me die in peace."

"Wake up, man!" Mike said. "She gave up everything for you."

"*What* are you talking about? Saving the theater is not giving up anything, and she didn't do it for me!"

Mike arched an eyebrow. "So you don't know?"

Ethan threw his palms in the air. "I guess I don't. I thought we weren't going to beat around the bush here. What else am I missing?"

"She quit the movie. Gave up the role."

Ethan jerked his head back. "What? When did she do that?"

"Does it matter? She did it *and* she did it for you."

Ethan rubbed the back of his neck. "She's going to end up resenting me. She can't do that."

"She already did."

Ethan ran a hand through his hair and blew out a deep breath. "Why didn't she mention any of this while she was here? That would've changed my perspective!"

Mike shrugged. "She probably wanted to see how you felt about her from the heart without bringing up external things, since you like things to happen *naturally*." He had to finish the sentence with air quotes.

Uncle Al opened his mouth again to speak.

Ethan held up his palm. "Wait! Don't say anything." He pointed to both Mike and Uncle Al. "Give me a moment here."

Ethan did laps around the kitchen island, deep in thought. His head was spinning from these new revelations. Sophia had quit the movie she was working on. Then she saved the theater. Then she came back to him, apologized, and almost begged him for another chance.

And he turned her away.

His chest tightened and all of a sudden he didn't feel so good. "What have I done?"

"You screwed up," Uncle Al said.

"I screwed up."

"Big time."

Mike made his way around the island and put his arm around Ethan. "Lucky for you I have a solution."

"Tell me."

Mike pulled out his cell phone. He made a few taps on the screen and handed the phone to Ethan, grinning.

Ethan used his thumb and index finger to zoom in on the document. "A boarding pass? You bought me a flight to Los Angeles?"

"No. I bought *us* flights. I want to see Chelsea while we're down there. Find someone to fill in for your ski lessons

251

tomorrow. Uncle Al is going to take care of Bear. Violet is going to stay at her grandmother's so I'm covered. *We* are going to Hollywood and *you* will get that woman back!"

<<<>>>

Later that evening, Mike pulled the rental car up to the front gate of a colonial-style mansion in Beverly Hills. There was a large circular driveway that could fit at least twenty cars. Palm trees circled the entire property.

Mike punched the security code into the keypad and the gate opened.

"Holy crap," Ethan said, shaking his head. "This place is unbelievable."

"I agree," Mike said, pulling the car around the driveway toward the front door.

Ethan shook his head in disbelief. "Hollywood's biggest movie star wants to be with me."

"Hell yeah, she does. I told you before; *you* deserve the best."

"Are you sure she's here?"

"Of course. I happen to be in love with her sister who lives around the corner." He winked and slapped Ethan on the leg. "Call me if you need anything, okay? I'll be close by."

"Okay. And . . . thank you."

"That's what friends are for."

Ethan rang the doorbell and waited.

Sophia opened the door, surprised.

Ethan was *more* surprised, seeing her makeup smeared. She'd been crying.

Now he felt like an even bigger idiot since he was the one who had caused those tears.

He reached up and brushed a tear from each side of her face. "It kills me to see you sad. I'm sorry."

"I'm the one who's sorry. I'm crying because I saw how much I hurt you."

"Why didn't you tell me you saved the theater? Or that you gave up your role in the movie?"

Sophia sniffled and studied him for a moment. "Would it have made a difference?"

"I'm on your doorstep in Beverly Hills. What do you think?"

She nodded but didn't reply.

"You can't quit that movie," Ethan said. "Call the studio and get your part back. I don't want you to have any regrets. We can figure out a way to make this work."

Sophia's bottom lip quivered. "Come in."

He followed her inside and stopped on the marble floor in the foyer, looking around. "Are you sure this isn't a hotel?"

"Very funny. Okay, I admit it's big." She fidgeted with her hands. "Follow me."

They went around the corner and down a hallway, entering the first room on the right.

Ethan stepped inside behind Sophia. It was the master

bedroom. The room was the size of both his family room and kitchen combined and had a king-sized bed against the center wall.

Sophia pointed to the leather purses that were piled high on the bed. "I'm giving them all away. Next I'm going to go through all my shoes."

He walked over and picked up one of the purses, inspecting it. "You don't need to give them up for me. I was just making a point."

"It's okay. I want to." She bit her lower lip. "I won't need them in Lake Tahoe if you take me back."

Ethan blinked, then a smile slowly formed on his face. "When you came to see me I was protecting myself, but there was something I wanted to do bad."

"What?"

"This." He wrapped his hands around her waist, pulled her against his body and kissed her.

Sophia caressed the side of his face. "No need to protect yourself. I won't ever hurt you again. I promise."

Ethan kissed her on each cheek and then on the lips. "As long as you're making promises, can I ask for one more thing?"

"Of course. Anything."

"Promise to let me win the next time we play pool."

Sophia poked him in the chest. "Don't be ridiculous."

"Stubborn."

She poked him again. "Pushy."

Kiss Me in the Snow

"You can't hurt me. I'm Superman, remember?"

They enjoyed a laugh and Ethan pulled her close again. "I love you."

Sophia sighed. "That's what I wanted to hear more than anything. I love you, too. I still can't believe you're here."

Ethan nodded. "Mark Twain said, 'To obtain the air the angels breathe, you must go to Tahoe.' For *me* to obtain the air that angels breathe, I just need to be wherever *you* are."

Epilogue

Eleven months later . . .

Violet pulled the red velvet curtain open a couple of inches and took another peek at the people seated on the other side. She let go of the curtain and sighed.

Something was wrong, but Sophia had no idea what.

It couldn't have been nerves because Violet had been in front of much larger groups than this. Last year's final performance of *A Charlie Brown Christmas* had had almost two hundred people in attendance. Over three hundred people had watched Violet take her acting craft to a smashing new level in the summer performance of *Anne of Green Gables*. Today's attendance wasn't even close to either of those.

Sophia put her arm around Violet. "You okay?"

Violet crinkled her nose. "I'm a little nervous." She pulled the curtain open again. "See the boy in the second row with the blue sweater and the green tie?"

Sophia took a look and nodded. "Yeah. He played Gilbert in *Anne of Green Gables*. Nicholas, right?"

"Yeah. Nicholas Taylor."

"Okay . . ."

"He's cute."

Sophia smiled.

It looked like someone had her first crush.

So sweet . . .

Sophia rubbed Violet's back. "You'll be fine. You were perfect at the rehearsal last night. We're just about ready to go. Break a leg."

"Thanks."

The DJ played "Trumpet Voluntary" by the Royal Philharmonic Orchestra. A few seconds later the wedding coordinator slid open the curtain.

Sophia walked down the makeshift aisle in the middle of the Heavenly Ballroom, the same location where they had had the amazing New Year's celebration almost a year earlier. She admired the strings of white lights overhead that connected to a giant heart in the middle of the room instead of the LED cube that counted down to midnight.

Sophia arrived at the white arbor and turned around to face the guests. She glanced over at Ethan, who looked handsome—delicious—in his black tuxedo. He winked at her and her heart skipped a beat. She thought how lucky she was to have such a wonderful man in her life.

Sophia smiled at Ethan, then glanced back down the aisle as Violet approached, tossing red rose petals.

Chelsea approached next, escorted by their dad, Mark. The guests rose as she approached her husband-to-be, the man with the biggest smile in the room. Chelsea looked as beautiful as ever in her vintage white wedding dress with subtle sequins and opalescent pearls.

The ceremony was beautiful and touching, and Sophia was honored to be the maid of honor.

After the cocktail hour, the guests sat for dinner. Ethan, Sophia, Chelsea, Mike, and Uncle Al talked about all the wonderful things that had happened over the last year.

The biggest changes were for Sophia and Chelsea, since both of them had moved to Lake Tahoe. Sophia had sold her mansion in Beverly Hills earlier in the year, moving in with Ethan and his goofy, lovable dog Bear. She was also the new artistic director of the conservatory theater and led their on-camera acting workshops and immersion programs.

And the good news didn't stop there. Sophia had signed a contract to star in *Lady Karma 4* on the condition it would be shot in Lake Tahoe. She'd also negotiated for Violet to have a small role in the movie. Sophia was the happiest she'd ever been in her life.

Uncle Al raised his glass. "To Mike and Chelsea."

"To Mike and Chelsea," everyone repeated.

Uncle Al cleared his throat. "I think it would be fitting if we all made our Christmas wishes right now."

Sophia thought back to last year and her wish of wanting an Academy Award.

Funny how things had changed.

"I'll start," Uncle Al said. "My Christmas wish is for Mike and Chelsea to have a baby next year."

"Uncle Al!" Chelsea said, sitting up in her seat. "You can't wish that."

"I already did," he said, chuckling and gesturing to Ethan.

"I can't wish for anything," Ethan said, squeezing Sophia's hand. "Everything in my life is perfect."

"That's a copout. Give us a wish."

Ethan nodded. "Fine. I also wish for Mike and Chelsea to have a baby."

"Me, too," Sophia said, clapping her hands.

"I'm game," Mike said, grinning.

Chelsea smacked Mike on the arm playfully. "I thought we were going to wait a little bit."

"Is a week long enough?"

"Hang on," Sophia said, noticing Violet was quiet. "Violet hasn't made her wish."

"That's true," Chelsea said, reaching over and rubbing Violet on the arm. "What do you wish for?"

"My wishes already came true," Violet answered. "I wanted you to be my mom and Lady Karma to be my aunt."

"That is so sweet, but since those already happened you need to make another wish."

"Okay," she said, thinking. "I would like a baby brother."

"Yes!" Uncle Al crowed, as laughter and smiles filled the table.

"This is a conspiracy, I tell you," Chelsea said, shaking her head.

Sophia leaned into Chelsea. "This has been the best year ever. I'm so happy for you."

"Thank you. You know I always wanted a Christmas wedding."

"And you got it."

The DJ played festive holiday music and Sophia sat up and turned to Ethan when she heard the start of "Last Christmas" by Wham!

"Looks like they're playing our song," Ethan said, standing and holding out his hand.

Sophia looked around the room at the guests who were finishing up their meals. "It's not time for dancing yet."

He grinned. "Come on, shy girl. Live a little."

She hesitated then took his hand, heading to the dance floor. "You're pushy."

Ethan spun Sophia around and pulled her close. "Well, you already know what *you* are."

"I know. Stubborn."

"*And* beautiful." Ethan kissed her. "The most beautiful woman in the room, as usual."

"How many times do I have to tell you?" asked Mike, scooting closer to Sophia and Ethan, dancing with his wife. "Chelsea is the most beautiful woman ever."

Sophia sighed. "Not this again. Can't we be tied?"

"No," Ethan and Mike said at the same time.

Later Chelsea and Mike cut the cake and the DJ announced there was also a dessert table.

Uncle Al headed over there with Ethan and Sophia, pointing to the pumpkin pie. "Did you know over one hundred million Americans have eaten pie for breakfast?"

"I would be one of them," a woman said, placing a stack of napkins on the table. "Here's something even more fascinating. Six million men every year have eaten the last slice of pie and denied it."

Uncle Al grinned. "*I* would be one of *them*."

The woman arched an eyebrow. "Who are you?"

"Everyone around here knows me as Uncle Al. You can call me Al."

"Is that a Paul Simon reference?"

"If it impresses you, yes."

"I'm Georgia," she said, shaking his hand. "I'm impressed you know so much about pies."

"I eat *a lot* of them."

The woman laughed.

"What's your excuse?"

"I bake them," Georgia said, smiling proudly. "I just moved here from Sacramento and opened a bakery next to Naked Fish Sushi. Plus, I'm on the board of the American Pie Council."

Uncle Al blinked twice. "I had no idea there was an American Pie Council."

"Oh, yeah. We're huge." She winked. "Come find me later and I'll fill you in."

"I'll do that."

Uncle Al watched the woman walk away, his mouth open.

Sophia whispered into Uncle Al's ear. "I think you've found your soulmate."

The DJ announced that Chelsea would toss the bouquet. Sophia headed to the middle of the dance floor along with five other single women.

Ethan cheered Sophia on from the side. "Keep your eye on the prize. You've got this."

"Get ready, ladies!" said the DJ. "Three, two, one, go!"

The women bumped bodies, jockeying for position as Chelsea swung her arm over her shoulder and hurled the bouquet up over the hanging heart in the middle of the room.

Sophia cut through two women and jumped as high as she could, snagging the bouquet out of the air with one hand.

"Yes!" Ethan said, running to the dance floor. He leaned down and kissed her, then picked her up and spun her around.

Sophia raised an eyebrow. "You do recall what it means when someone catches the bouquet, right?"

He pulled her close. "Hell yeah, I do. And if I had it my way I would have grabbed the bouquet from Chelsea and handed it to you to prove my point."

Sophia smiled and kissed him on the lips, anticipating a proposal coming soon.

She couldn't wait to be his wife.

They walked off the dance floor and Sophia pointed to the window. "It's snowing!"

Ethan chuckled. "You never get tired of it."

"Never." She pulled Ethan by the hand toward the coat check. "Come on. Let's grab our jackets."

"Now? Why?"

She stopped and placed her hands on her hips. "You should know the routine by now."

"You mean . . .?"

She nodded. "Kiss me in the snow."

THE END

<<<<>>>

Acknowledgements

Dear Reader,

I hope you enjoyed *Kiss Me in the Snow*. I certainly had a lot of fun writing it! This book is very special to me because it's my very first Christmas romantic comedy. Now I'm motivated to write many more!

I would just like to take a moment to thank you for your support. Without you, I would not be able to write romantic comedies for a living. I love your emails and communication on Facebook and Twitter. You motivate me to write faster! Don't be shy. Send an email to me at rich@richamooi.com to say hello. I personally respond to all emails and would love to hear from you.

Please leave a review of the book on Amazon and Goodreads! I appreciate it very much and it will help new readers find my stories.

It takes more than a few people to publish a book so I want to send out a big THANK YOU to everyone who helped make *Kiss Me in the Snow* possible.

First, thank you to my hot Spanish wife, <u>Silvi Martin</u>. She's the first person to read my stories and always gives me amazing feedback to make them better. I love you, my angel.

To my cover artist, Sue Traynor, for drawing another beautiful cover.

To my assistant, Mary Guidry. Thank you for all that you do.

Thanks to Mary Yakovets for editing and to Paula Bothwell for proofreading.

Special thanks to my beta readers, Maché, Robert, Krasimir, and Julita. You rock! You help me transform the story into something more entertaining. You're the best!

Thanks to Hannah Jayne, the super secret AC author group, Chick Lit Chat, Romance Writers of America, RWA Silicon Valley, the Le Bou Bunch, and the Indie Author Collective.

With gratitude from the bottom of my heart.

Rich

P.S. Don't worry, be happy! :)

Made in the USA
Charleston, SC
07 February 2017